THE ACCIDENTAL SPY

I0676737

A Nick Andrews Novel

Book 1

By

Jack Durish

2nd Edition

Revised & Updated Edition

Rewritten. Reloaded.

The Accidental Spy

A Nick Andrews Novel

Book 1

By

Jack Durish

2nd Edition

Published by Jack Durish

ISBN: 979-8-9995767-3-6

Cover art and author portrait by Mark Jordan

Visit Mark at MarkJordanPhoto.com

Author's Note & Disclaimer

This is a work of historical fiction. While it is grounded in real events and features the names of historical figures, many characters, conversations, and situations have been fictionalized or dramatized for narrative purposes.

The portrayal of real individuals—living or deceased—such as political leaders, public figures, and cultural icons, is entirely imaginative and not intended to represent actual events, beliefs, or actions with historical accuracy. Any resemblance to actual persons, living or dead, in unintended contexts is purely coincidental.

Where possible, historical events and timelines have been respected. However, for the sake of storytelling, certain liberties have been taken with chronology, geography, and dialogue. This novel should not be relied upon as a factual source but rather as an exploration of history through a creative lens.

Table of Contents

Preface

The world in 1947 is brittle, balanced on the edge of a new kind of war. Europe lies in ruin. The Soviet Union tightens its grip on Eastern Europe. In Greece and Turkey, communist insurgents push hard. Fear travels faster than freight in postwar ports.

Truman steps before Congress in March. His voice is clear, his words unyielding: the United States will support free peoples resisting subjugation by armed minorities or outside pressures. It's a doctrine born not just of ideology, but of exhaustion— American exhaustion with war, with appeasement, with watching others fall. The message is simple: the spread of communism must end. The containment line is drawn.

But that line is hazy. Not by design, but by diplomacy. The Soviets test it in Berlin. Mao redraws it in China. And in Korea, divided and festering since the Japanese surrender, the powder settles. North and South glare at each other across the 38th Parallel. U.S. troops are gone now. The South is weak, corrupt, vulnerable. But no one says it aloud.

It's January 1950. The San Francisco Press Club hums with the casual murmur of seasoned reporters and polished government men. Dean Acheson, Truman's Secretary of State, takes the podium. The room leans in. He outlines America's Pacific defense perimeter — Japan, the Ryukyus, and the Philippines. A string of islands like buoys in the sea of postwar uncertainty.

But he doesn't mention Korea.

He doesn't say the United States will defend it.

No one gasps. No one flinches. The omission is quiet, almost elegant in its subtlety. But across the ocean, in Moscow, and later in Pyongyang, the silence is deafening. Stalin reads it as permission. Kim Il-sung reads it as an invitation. The match is struck.

And the gunpowder of Korea — long spilled, long dry — begins to burn.

#

The Army taught him to be a Ranger.
A warrior teaches him to kill.

CHAPTER ONE

Dropped Into the Fire

Nick Andrews grew up during World War II playing soldiers. All he knows of war comes from John Wayne and Randolph Scott movies and the newsreels that accompanied them. Those in his family, others who lived in his community or attended his church – those who experienced it – never spoke of it. Nothing they could have told him resembled the war he was born to fight.

To Private First-Class Nick Andrews – Airborne, Ranger -- the Korean War doesn't unfold like the conflicts his drill instructors had warned him about. It comes fast, violent, and without clear borders. It sweeps the length of the Korean Peninsula twice, from the Yalu River to the Pusan Perimeter and back before he'd even arrived – all in the span of little more than six months.

General MacArthur had won the battle against the North Koreans with a brilliant and daring invasion at Inchon that cut their supply lines and left their army as fallen fruit to be gathered at leisure.

Nick didn't enlist to fight. He enlisted to escape a malignantly abusive father and maybe earn G.I. Benefits to further his education. And he might never have had to fight if MacArthur had contented himself to stand within a stone's throw of China and savor his victory. He didn't. He chooses to give voice to an ambition to drive communism out of China, with nuclear weapons if necessary.

President Truman orders MacArthur to return to Washington to explain himself, but the General disobeys, forcing the President to fly to him.

That's when Nick arrives in Korea at the request of his Ranger Drill Instructor. The DI wants Nick to join a Ranger Reconnaissance Platoon that MacArthur is sending to the Yalu River to ascertain the intentions of the Chinese Communist Peoples (CCP) Army, to support his argument with the President.

The other members of the platoon, all World War II veterans, resent Nick's presence on the mission. They had learned to resent replacements during World War II, and habits learned in combat are hard to break. However, Nick is no ordinary replacement.

Nick has exceptional skills as a navigator. He learned to sail and navigate on Chesapeake Bay and in navigator competitions along the East Coast. His Ranger School DI had never seen his like and, as the ranking member of the team, insists that everyone give Nick a chance.

They give Nick better than a chance. They kick him out of the door of the C-47 Dakota first on the night when the platoon parachutes on top of the CCP column crossing the Yalu. Being first, Nick lands on one side of the column before the platoon is spotted. He is the only one to survive.

#

CHAPTER TWO

Lost With Only the Memory of a Map

Nick arrives in Korea with a pocket full of maps. None are drawn on a scale useful for navigating, but they provide him with an overview of the peninsula's topography that proves invaluable to his survival.

North and South Korea share the same peninsula that separates the Yellow Sea and the Sea of Japan. The two nations are joined at a line that meanders between them along the 38th Parallel of latitude.

The eastern side of the peninsula is dominated by a spine of mountains known as the Taebaek Mountains, which run roughly north to south parallel to the Sea of Japan (East Sea). These steep ranges rise abruptly from the coastline, giving eastern Korea a dramatic terrain of narrow valleys and ridges. The highest peak, Mount Paektu (2,744 meters / 9,003 feet), straddles the border with China in the north and is both a geographic and cultural icon—believed by some traditions to be the mythical birthplace of the Korean people. The Americans who fight in these mountains will forever after remember, "Behind every mountain is another mountain."

In contrast, the western side of the Korean Peninsula slopes gently toward the Yellow Sea, featuring broad river plains, rolling hills, and fertile deltas—particularly the Han River basin around Seoul and the Geum River further south. These areas support much of the country's agriculture and population centers, especially in South Korea.

The Yalu River separates North Korea from China, and the Taedong River flows westward from the mountains in the east to the Yellow Sea in the west after passing through the nation's capital, Pyongyang. South Korea's capital, Seoul, and Pyongyang are separated by a mere 121 miles.

∞

From the shadowed folds of the foothills north of the Taedong River about two-thirds of the distance from the Yalu River to the 38th Parallel, Nick lies prone beneath a thicket of frostbitten brush, his breath shallow, his belly hollow. The night air is frigid, the wind still. Below him, the valley unfurls like a theater of war lit by a pale wash of moonlight and the dim flicker of lanterns.

A pontoon bridge stretches across the wide, sluggish Taedong like a crooked stitch, swaying gently with each shuffle of heavily laden porters. Over it streams a seemingly endless line of peasants — men, women, and bent-backed teenagers — each bearing crates, bundles, and sacks heavier than their frames should allow. They move in silence, save for the muted splash of boots in the waterlogged planks and the occasional bark of a Chinese soldier keeping the column in motion.

North of the river, a battered freight train sits idle, its cars disgorging supplies in chaotic stacks. Soldiers and porters pass crates hand to hand, some marked with stenciled Chinese characters, others barely held together by wire and rope. South of the river, the cargo disappears into the black mouths of other freight cars guarded by soldiers manning machine guns on the roofs of each and praying that they won't have to use them.

Once their loads are deposited, the peasants are forced to return and carry another – and another. It is a circus of torment with death its only escape.

A little upstream, the skeletal remains of a railway bridge rise from the water like broken ribs of an ancient, drowned beast. Steel girders twisted and collapsed under bombardment not long past, its decking torn away by fire and fury. Rust-colored stains bleed from the wreckage into the current, and a shattered boxcar lies half-submerged on the southern bank — a grim reminder of battles and failed retreats.

As Nick watches, he knows that the Chinese and North Koreans are chasing the UN forces further south. He must move soon, cross this river, or never catch up and pass them to rejoin his Army.

Swimming isn't an option. He could make it easily during the summer, but this is Korea, where winter comes early, and the water is waiting to kill him as surely as an enemy bullet.

He could walk upriver to find another crossing, how far he doesn't know, and down the river is Pyongyang. It's close enough that the outskirts of the enemy capital can be seen during the day, even without binoculars.

No, he must cross the pontoon bridge, and the only way across is disguised as a peasant.

Peasant clothing is no great problem. There are plenty of dead and frozen peasants of every sex, size, and shape littering the countryside. All he has to do is find one and swap clothes. The difference in his skin tone and facial structure shouldn't be a problem either. His filth – gathered from his 200-mile trek without adequate shelter and no bathing – should camouflage his differences. He even has a plan for overcoming his lack of familiarity with the Korean language. He'll pretend that he's a deaf mute if anyone attempts to converse with him.

The only insurmountable impediment that Nick can foresee is his lack of strength. Physically, he's not spent, not entirely. Emotionally and morally, that's another matter. Alone and lost in an alien world, he can't even imagine succeeding.

Nick has long suspected that he is a coward. Growing up with an abusive father shaped him. Whereas his older brother would stand up and fight their father – a man who had escaped the coalmines of Pennsylvania as a prizefighter – Nick hid. Nick didn't realize his brother was trying to protect him, and his brother didn't know it wasn't necessary.

Whatever his strengths and limitations, Nick is determined to try. He has no other option. Every other straggler he saw who surrendered was murdered. If shot, it is a blessing. However, most have been murdered slowly, cruelly.

No, he must try to cross the bridge.

Nick shuffles among the dead and frozen remains of refugees – peasants mostly. Most were thin and cadaverous before they died. So is Nick in life. Months in infantry training, followed by Airborne and Ranger Schools, stripped him of his baby fat. Months straggling behind the CCP army stripped him of the muscle he wishes he still had. Height is his only concern as he surveys the scattered corpses – few are as tall as he.

Wandering the field of the dead, Nick wonders – "How did they come to be here?"

Nick is the child of Western Civilization and American education. He believes that cause breeds effect, inspiring a new question: "What did they do to deserve this?"

When he finds suitable peasant clothing, he is loath to wear it, fearing that an Angel of Death might mistake him for one who deserves to die. The philosophy of the absurdity or incomprehensibility of existence has not yet ensnared him.

He spends far too much time and energy pondering these questions before concluding that these peasants have simply been forced into the same narrow corridors as the vying armies and the land.

#

CHAPTER THREE

A Corpse Among the Living

Nick is almost ready to make his attempt to cross the pontoon bridge disguised as a Korean peasant. He has only to equip himself with a wooden A-frame that the peasants use to carry loads on their backs and to choose which personal possession he shall take or leave behind.

The first choices are easy. He must leave behind anything that will expose him as an American soldier – no, an American spy. He is no longer in uniform. This awareness causes him to laugh at its absurdity. American soldier or spy makes no difference; the punishment is the same, and he is forced to surrender his M1 Garand and ammunition, helmet, and boots. He hides these beneath the peasant who donated his clothes to Nick's disguise.

He hides his binoculars and compass under the peasant garb. He straps his bayonet and its sheath to his ankle, under his trouser leg.

Last, his most valuable treasure is hidden inside his jacket – his Rutter.

Nick began keeping a Rutter since he started sailing at the age of thirteen. It's his diary of all the places he sailed – on the Chesapeake Bay, the Atlantic Coast, and the Caribbean. It contains personal notes on his observations of winds and tides, wave characteristics, water temperatures, and salinity. It includes sketches of unusual coastal features, aids to navigation, and harbor entrances. And it contains routes taken. The name Rutter is derived from the French for "route". He learned about them while studying ancient mariners who used them before accurate charts were available.

He's been using it to record his observations since he landed at the Yalu River. Along the way south, he's noted enemy bivouacs and routes of march as well as the locations of ammunition, supply, and fuel dumps.

As soon as he realized that America and its allies controlled the skies over the Korean Peninsula, he understood why the CCP army always moved at night and rested during the day. The military intelligence that has been accumulating in his Rutter will be invaluable if he can deliver it to UN commanders. It has become his *raison d'être* – his reason for surviving. Without it, he might already have surrendered to the elements, if not the enemy.

∞

Prepared, Nick makes his way down the slope just after dusk to join the line of peasants accepting their loads at the nearest boxcar. He keeps his head down and his face covered in the early evening, allowing himself to be jostled and shoved by the CCP guards.

He's backed up against the side of the boxcar at the door and forced to wait while workers inside load his backpack and lash the supplies in place.

When the loader shouts something in Korean, a guard grabs him by the arm and shoves Nick towards the end of the line headed for the bridge.

The line shuffles to the near end of the bridge, where a guard shouts something to each peasant before they step onto it. When it's Nick's turn, he nods and grunts and steps onto the bridge out of step with the person ahead of him, surmising that the peasants are being warned that walking in step will cause the bridge to undulate until they are thrown off.

So far, so good.

When Nick steps off on the far shore, he is almost convinced that he will be safe until one of the peasants ahead of him falters and falls from exhaustion. Before a guard notices, another peasant kneels and tries to help. Nick is almost past when the second peasant begins pleading with Nick in Korean.

Nick attempts to shuffle past, but the peasant reaches out and grabs his wrist. The grip is surprisingly strong, and he can't pull away. Out of reflex, Nick looks down, and his eyes meet those of the peasant hanging onto him.

It's a woman, and she gasps.

"You're an American."

It's not a question. It's a statement.

Nick recoils in fear and pulls free, but the woman grabs his wrist again, stronger this time.

She lowers her voice.

"Help me."

Only then does Nick realize that she's speaking English. Expecting Korean, he can't understand the words.

"Help me."

#

CHAPTER FOUR

The Woman Speaks English

The woman's words ricochet through Nick's head. He shakes his head desperately and realizes that his reflex belies his ruse of deafness.

She pleads again.

Nick looks from side to side, searching for an escape. Fortunately, no guards are looking in Nick's direction.

When he looks back down at the woman, she is helping the peasant who collapsed to shrug off her pack. Nick takes the opportunity to begin shuffling away, but the woman rises and catches him.

"Help me and I'll help you."

Nick turns back and grabs the A-frame now leaning against the fallen peasant and begins threading her arms back into the shoulder straps.

The file of refugees continues trudging past, too lost in their misery to notice anything. Even the snatches of foreign words fall on deaf ears.

"What are you doing?"

Nick ignores her and continues to remount the A-frame on the woman's back.

"She has to deliver the load. We can't take it for her, and we can't leave her here, can we?"

"But she can't carry it."

"We'll help, one on each side."

21

Nick helps the woman to her feet as the English-speaking woman translates the plan into Korean. The three of them rejoin the file, shuffling towards the train where the supplies are being reloaded. Nick must bear the full weight of the woman's faltering body and his load until they reach the open door.

As soon as he's delivered his load, Nick attempts to shuffle away, but he attracts the attention of a guard who intercepts him and uses his rifle to shove Nick back in line.

The woman appears at Nick's side and says something to the guard, who shoves both on their way back to the bridge.

"We must go back to carry another load."

"How many?"

"Until the train over there is empty."

"What happened to the woman we helped?"

"I convinced the guard that she only needed a little rest."

The report of a rifle firing startles everyone. Looking back in the direction of the sound, Nick sees the woman they helped on the ground twitching in death throes. The guard standing over her lowers his rifle.

When Nick turns back, the woman beside him is weeping silently.

The file backs up at the bridge, where a guard there instructs each peasant on how to cross safely. While they wait, the guttural roar of a rotary piston engine attracts everyone's attention. Nick looks up and sees the underbelly of a Navy A-4 Skyraider passing overhead. Its wing racks are bristling with rockets, and the bomb that it dropped a split-second earlier is arching towards the center of the bridge. He turns back and dives, landing on top of his new companion.

The bomb explodes with a roar muffled by water rising in a column near the center of the bridge and then raining down on all sides.

Screams of hysteria mingle with sounds of pain and bodies falling into the river. Bubbles rise to the surface, marking where many jumped into the river and struggled to free themselves from their backpacks until they drowned.

Nick rises to his feet with his companion in tow and races back to the railway. He doesn't have to see that other Skyraiders are following the first and that there will be more bombs. The flight will then wheel and return with rocket and cannon fire until the bridge and the trains are destroyed. These planes carry an incredible amount of ordnance and fuel enough to linger on target until the job is done.

Nick releases the woman and runs to the train, which is already beginning to move slowly towards a tunnel for shelter while the gunners on the roof of each boxcar fire their weapons at the warplanes. They have no time to worry about anyone on the ground.

A broken box of grenades lay on the ground where it was dropped when the attack began. He grabs two of the grenades, pulls their safety pins, and tosses them inside on a pile of artillery shells.

Nick throws himself under a toppled boxcar on another railway siding and braces himself against the stone roadbed.

The initial blast passes over Nick without harming him, but the heat of it sears across his back. It's the first warmth that he's felt in months.

Nick crawls from beneath the shelter of the crippled railcar and jumps to his feet. He knows that he must get away as far as possible or find another shelter before debris begins to rain back to Earth.

He appraises the roof of a warehouse as he passes and decides that it is safer inside than trying to outrun the debris. As he enters, he trips over a CCP guard lying on the floor in the fetal position with his rifle leaning against the wall nearby. He grabs the gun, and the guard flees outside into the path of a falling chunk of iron that decapitates him. He sets the rifle aside – it's too little to defend himself against a Chinese horde. As he shrugs out of his A-frame backpack to load it, another figure dives through the doorway. It is his companion.

Together, though not cooperatively, they search the closer stacks of supplies and find fifty-pound sacks of rice and bundles of blankets. Each loads a sack of rice and two blankets and tie them in place on their A-frame backpacks.

Nick glances outside and, seeing that the shower of debris has stopped, takes off running towards a town he spotted nearby.

He reaches it to discover that its population has fled, and he races to the far side. There is a ridge line about ten miles south of the town, and Nick is determined to reach it and find cover before the sun rises.

Nick slows his pace on the other side of the town, reducing it to a pace he believes that he can maintain until he reaches his goal. It is only then that he glances back and finds the woman following him. Although she is slowly falling behind, Nick still credits her endurance in that she has been able to follow him this far.

∞

The A-frame rides comfortably on Nick's back as he runs for another hour. He counts the paces and slips a knotted string between his fingers for each one hundred. Counting the knots and multiplying them times the length of his stride, he estimates that he has covered five miles since leaving the town's edge.

He then holds his hand at arm's length and sees that two fingers fill the space between the base and top of the hill towards which he is headed. Another estimate leads him to believe that he can reach the hill and scale it in another hour.

Again, he glances back but can't see anyone following him. However, the ground is rising, and anyone following may be able to see him silhouetted against the sky. He plans to be prepared to defend himself when he crests the hill in case he is being followed.

Nick makes camp as the dawn is breaking about an hour to the east, and he wants to conceal himself and cook some rice before it breaks overhead.

His rice is cooking in a discarded GI helmet over a hatful of fire when the woman arrives.

She joins him, and they eat without speaking.

When finished, Nick banks the fire and rolls up in his two blankets. The woman wraps hers around herself and lies down on the ground against Nick's back.

Nick begrudgingly admits that her closeness is comforting and warm.

#

CHAPTER FIVE

A Map of his Own

Nick ignores her presence when he awakens the next day, towards noon. After checking the surrounding countryside to ensure there is no one nearby, he takes out his Rutter and begins making observations.

The woman relieves herself in the bushes nearby, then returns to Nick's side, where she wraps herself in her blankets and sits.

Nick calculates that he had run southwest through the night based on his observations of the stars. He adds that he ran approximately 8 miles from the railway. To this, he adds his calculations of the hill's height where they now rested.

Lastly, Nick marks an "X" in the center of the page and an "N" at the top, denoting the compass direction to the North. He completes his preparations by adding a scale labeled "1 Mile" at the bottom of the page.

Laying his Rutter level on the ground, he orients the page with his compass so that the edge of the page points towards Magnetic North. Lying down, he sights over the "X" towards the ridgeline from which he had overserved the scene where the trains were packed. He places a "1" eight miles – according to his scale – from the "X". Now he begins sighting all distinctive landmarks surrounding their location with numbers. He can't estimate distances, but when compared to an accurately drawn map, he can determine precisely where the "X" would lie.

The woman watches him carefully as he works.

"You're making a map."

"Not exactly. They're observations that can help me locate this place accurately on a real map, if ever I get the chance."

"How long have you been doing this?"

"Ever since I was thirteen."

"No, I mean, where do these observations start?"

Nick looks at her appraisingly as if considering whether he should tell her.

"Ever since the Yalu River."

The woman reacts, startled.

"You've walked all the way here?"

"Yes. How far have you walked?"

The woman pauses as if considering her response.

"I was in Seoul when the war started, and we went to Pusan. Most of that was on a truck. We had to abandon the truck about fifty miles from Pusan and walked the rest of the way. After the landing at Inchon, we were taken by airplane back to Seoul."

"Why? What's in Seoul?"

"I was an intern at the Catholic hospital there."

"You're a doctor?"

"Almost."

"Where did you go next?"

"After the Chinese entered Seoul, we escaped on foot. We got as far as the Taedong River, where we met."

"That was the Taedong?"

"Yes."

Nick opens his Rutter back to the page where he had made his observations from the ridgeline.

After labeling the river, he turns back to his pages for the current location.

"Excuse me while I finish."

"Okay, but please, may I ask? What is your name?"

"Nick?"

"I'm Soon-Ja."

"It's nice to meet you, Soon-Ja."

Soon-Ja covers her mouth and giggles.

"What?"

"In Korea, the family name is first. My given name is Ja."

Nick fails to see the humor but nods that he understands.

He then returns to his book, making sketches of each numbered landmark and adding observations to each. He also sketches the lead Skyraider that bombed the bridge.

"You made a mistake."

Nick looks at Soon-Ja-ja, an unspoken question in his eyes.

"The number on the plane was '508', not '503'."

"You're sure?"

"Pretty sure."

Nick annotates the drawing.

Why is that important?

"The Navy will have records of that plane's location on the date and time I recorded. It will either confirm the accuracy of my calculations or an error factor that can be applied to my other calculations."

When finished, he glances at the Sun's position.

"It's about 1400 hours. That's 2 p.m."

"I understand the 24-hour clock."

"Okay. I'm going to get some more sleep. When I wake up, I'll cook some more rice and then be gone at dusk."

"Can I come with you?"

"I can't slow down?"

"Why?"

"I have to catch up with the CCP forward elements and break through to reach an American command."

"I haven't slowed you down yet."

Nick pauses to consider her answer.

"And I'll be going close to danger."

Soon-Ja laughs and extends her arms with her palms up.

"It's dangerous everywhere."

"Well, I can't be responsible for you."

"I'm not asking you to be responsible for me."

"Well, what are you asking for?"

Soon-Ja looks away demurely.

"I just want company. I've been scared ever since I left Seoul. I feel safer with someone."

Nick stands and paces while Soon-Ja watches him struggle with a decision until he returns.

"Okay. I guess I can't stop you without shooting you. But you must keep up."

Soon-Ja smiles in response, and Nick stares at her, appraising her chances.

\#

CHAPTER SIX

Marching With Shadows

Nick has traveled at night ever since he left the Yalu River. He reasoned that it was easiest to follow the Chinese, since they were headed in the direction he wanted to go. And if they were going to travel at night, that's when he would travel.

It seemed apparent to Nick that the Chinese moved their troops and supplies at night to avoid American warplanes that dominated the skies over Korea. What wasn't obvious was the reason they failed to post military police to guard their routes of march. Apparently, they were confident that American stragglers posed no threat to them.

Peasants move during the daylight hours to avoid the CCP army. When he was in uniform, there was a danger that peasants might seize him and turn him over to the Chinese for food and favors if he were traveling with them.

Now, they will more likely grab him and Soon-Ja to take their food and blankets.

Nick sees no reason to change his tactics. He and Soon-Ja will follow the CCP army at night.

∞

Nick awakens with a start. Soon-Ja isn't beside him. He staggers to his feet – not yet fully awake --

and finds her sitting beside a small, smokeless fire melting ice in the steel helmet.

"There isn't anyone nearby."

Nick isn't reassured until he looks for himself.

"There's smoke rising from beside the road about two miles south of us."

Nick looks in that direction and sees several columns of smoke.

"That must be one of their bivouacs."

Nick agrees and reaches for his Rutter. He plots a new location on his page and identifies it as "Bivouac?".

He turns to find Soon-Ja adding two handfuls of rice from her bag to the boiling water in the helmet. She's wearing a slight smile of satisfaction.

Nick reluctantly concedes that she may prove helpful.

"Thanks."

After each takes their portion of the rice, Soon-Ja cleans the helmet and begins melting more water to boil. To this, she adds shavings from a root she carries in a pouch hanging from her belt, then removes the helmet from the fire.

"What are you making?"

"Tea."

As the tea steeps in the helmet, they get to know each other.

"Where did you study medicine?"

"Georgetown University, that's in..."

"I know Georgetown. I'm from Maryland."

"How old are you, soldier?"

"Ranger."

Soon-Ja notes the pride in his voice.

"You know what that is?"

Soon-Ja nods in the affirmative.

"Why were you in Seoul?"

"I went to St. Mary's Hospital for my internship and to get married."

"You're married?"

Soon-Ja hesitates, and Nick guesses there's been a tragedy.

"He was killed when artillery hit St. Mary's."

"I'm sorry."

Soon-Ja smiles sadly.

"It's not as bad as it sounds. It's bad, and I'm sad, but it was an arranged marriage. I had only met him once."

"Sorry, I didn't know."

"You didn't know that arranged marriages were still a thing."

Nick blushes.

"They are in Korea and some other places."

∞

Nick and Soon-Ja cover all signs of their camp and head south towards the place where they see smoke. By the time they arrive, a battalion-sized group of CCP soldiers is leaving their bivouac and heading south.

Nick waits until the last of them rounds a bend in a road and stations Soon-Ja in the brush.

"I want to inspect their camp."

"Why?"

"I want to see if it's regularly used or just a place this group stopped at. You come and tell me if any other soldiers come this way."

Soon-Ja nods her understanding, and Nick disappears into the woods. He's gone for about half an hour before he returns.

Taking out his Rutter, he erases the question mark he had added to "Bivouac" and begins looking about.

"What are you looking for?"

"The bivouacs seem to be evenly spaced along their routes of march. I'm looking for some sign that troop commanders use to spot them. And supply truck drivers must be able to find them, too."

"There are supplies in there?"

"There were. There's enough trash for supplies that many troops have used, and they're not worried about cleaning up after themselves."

"What else is in there?"

"Not much. They've cut down most of the trees. Left enough to hold up the camouflage netting."

Nick resumes looking for some sort of sign with Soon-Ja helping him.

"Why don't they just leave guards to point the way?"

Nick loses himself in thought for several minutes before responding.

"That would seem reasonable. I don't know. I can't read their minds."

Nick and Soon-Ja survive in the gaps between marching Communist units and begin walking without resolving the issue. They chat about the problem as they walk side-by-side, dismissing each idea after careful consideration and debate.

After several miles, Soon-Ja notices Nick fidgeting with a knotted string.

"Are you praying?"

Nick regards her, bewildered, until she points to the string he holds.

"It reminds me of a rosary."

Nick chuckles.

"No, it just helps me keep track of the miles."

Soon-Ja's bewildered expression prompts Nick to explain.

"I'm counting my paces. Each knot represents twenty. There are ninety-three knots."

Nick hands her the string and continues his explanation while she studies it.

"The double knots represent quarter miles, and the triple knot represents one mile. I tally each mile in my Rutter with notes about the path we've been walking. I've learned through practice that my stride stretches ten percent when walking uphill. It shortens ten percent down steep hills."

"Could I relieve you? Pace off the miles?"

"Thanks, no. This is my mission, and accuracy is crucial. Besides, we don't have a way of measuring your stride."

#

CHAPTER SEVEN

The Road South

Nick and Soon-Ja walk through the night, listening to the troops marching ahead and frequently glancing back for signs of anyone approaching from behind.

Even in the dark, Soon-Ja can see that something is troubling Nick. After a convoy of trucks passes and they reenter the road, she is concerned that he is still distracted.

"What's troubling you?

Nick hesitates to respond.

"You can tell me?"

"Can I trust you?"

Soon-Ja laughs softly.

"You should have decided that by now."

Nick smiles to himself.

"I don't know if I can, but I want to."

"Why?"

"It helps to talk out problems. It's an old habit of mine. Whenever something bothers me, I pace and talk to myself or someone else."

Having not heard a question, Soon-Ja remains silent.

"It's just that traffic is diminishing the farther we get from China."

"So?"

"It should be increasing."

"Why?"

"Troops closer to the front have greater needs. They've walked further."

"So, they need more calories."

"Exactly. And troops at the front need ammunition. Lots of ammunition."

"So, what are you thinking?"

"I think that our forces are falling back, concentrating their position and shortening their lines of supply, while the CCP is overreaching theirs."

"But we've seen signs of battle already."

"Skirmishes designed to delay the CCP. Make them deploy for battle and then regroup before they can resume marching."

Soon-Ja studies Nick as he speaks.

"You have a problem with that?"

"No, I was just thinking that you're talking like someone with a lot more experience than a private or corporal should have."

"Private. I've read a lot of history."

"Military history?"

"All kinds of history. It was my favorite subject in school. It's what I want to study in college."

"You want to go to college."

"Yes. I'm hoping that I'll have GI benefits like the World War II veterans."

"Your family can't help?"

"My father wouldn't help if he could."

"Well, you should study what you love, and it's obvious that you love history."

Behind them, the sound of gears clashing and motors roaring makes their heads turn. Although lights aren't visible, they prepare to leave the road until the convoy passes.

"That's what, the third tonight?"

"Yes, and it's almost dawn. I used to see as many as ten every night."

Soon-Ja thinks about what Nick has told her as the convoy passes.

"Is it possible that they're using a different route to bring supplies?"

"No."

"Why not?"

"The land won't permit it."

Soon-Ja's expression tells Nick that he'll have to expand on his explanation.

"The CCP has two places where they can ship supplies to Korea. They can ship them by land to crossings on the Yalu River, or by sea. Well, not by sea, not really."

"Why not?"

"China doesn't have the naval forces to protect the few sea routes to the West Coast of Korea, and Russia doesn't either to protect shipping to the East Coast. No, almost everything must come across the Yalu River, and there are very few land routes south from the Yalu."

"You sound like you have a thing for maps, too."

"I'm also a sailor."

"And you're not in the Navy?"

"No, and that's another story."

Ahead, Nick has spotted the convoy turning off the main road.

"It's almost dawn and it looks like they're going into hiding for the day."

"I guess that means we will, too."

"Yes."

#

CHAPTER EIGHT

Panthers in the Valley

After selecting their campsite for the day and having their meal of tea and rice supplemented by two rats that Nick snares, he goes in search of the convoy parked on the other side of the road. He finds them huddled together under a vast camouflage net covering a bivouac with another convoy and the troops that Nick and Soon-Ja had been trailing.

"Well, at least these guys will eat well today."

He's surprised there aren't any guards posted, giving him a chance to sneak onto a few of the trucks and inventory what they are hauling. All seemed to be loaded with fuel and ammunition.

"Maybe they won't be eating so well today."

Nick catches himself talking aloud and thinks to himself.

"I have to stop doing that."

∞

Back at camp, Nick finds Soon-Ja still awake.

"Great, you're awake. We're going to split up tomorrow."

Soon-Ja reacts in a panic before Nick can finish.

"No, no! It's only temporary. You can follow the troops tomorrow night. The convoys, there are two of them parked there, will probably leave first. If they don't just leave after the trucks and follow the road until daylight. I'll find you."

"Where are you going?"

"There's a narrow valley ahead. I'm going to climb the western rim and follow it. That'll give me vantage points to fix my position better."

"How will you find me?"

"I'll tell you when I do."

Soon-Ja is not comforted by Nick's promise and is not happy spending her first day alone after he leaves.

∞

Nick climbs the western rim because it provides better cover and concealment than the opposite side of the valley. Once on top, he opens his Rutter to a fresh page and draws another reference diagram. This is one of the best he's had to fix his location on a real map when and if he ever can sit down with one.

While there, he hears a familiar sound in the underbrush and goes in search of it. Ten minutes later, he is gutting and plucking a chicken, smiling when he thinks of how happy Soon-Ja will be. When he's finished, he hears another sound, also familiar. Even though he doesn't understand the language, he recognizes the sentiment. A sergeant is very angry with some private, likely the one who allowed the chicken to escape.

As Nick melts away into the underbrush – the bird bound at its shanks and hanging from his sash –

he's very glad that he buried the offal and feathers and concealed its grave.

∞

The CCP convoys and troops dash out of hiding before sunset that night. The roar of their trucks awakens Soon-Ja, and she watches them all depart. She hesitates to follow them but fears being left too far behind.

She breaks camp, concealing all signs of it, and advances cautiously to the road. After half an hour of waiting, she steps onto the road and follows at a brisk pace.

In the distance, she hears a roar – a different kind of roar. Moments later, a sleek U.S. Navy jet sweeps overhead with a trail of tracers chasing it.

Nick watches from above when the first trucks enter the valley. It doesn't take long to discern their purpose. He had already seen anti-aircraft batteries below him on both sides of the valley. Convoys and troops reaching this point in their march south were meant to be decoys, to lure the American warplanes into a trap.

As the first Panther jet roars past about fifty feet below his vantage point, the antiaircraft batteries open fire. Nick can only hope and pray that Soon-Ja wasn't suckered into following them.

∞

Soon-Ja dives for cover in a culvert passing under the road as soon as the first Panther jet streaks overhead. She trembles in the dark as the sound of the next two pummels her. Troops are also diving for cover, but they are several hundred yards further south.

It is the sound of the fourth Panther jet that truly terrifies her as it almost crashes on the road directly above her, causing a storm of concrete dust to rain down and cover her. Still, she remains in the culvert thinking it is safer than being in the open, especially when she hears shouts from the Chinese running to make sure the pilot is dead and to see if anything valuable can be recovered from the wreckage.

Soon-Ja looks in the direction of their voices and is terrified to see burning jet fuel pooling at the open end of the culvert. She turns to crawl away until she sees the legs of someone running past the other open end of the culvert. Given the choice of being captured or burning to death, Soon-Ja chooses the former when the pool of burning fuel rises above the bottom lip of the culvert and begins to creep towards her, and she scrambles away from it.

When she reaches the end of the culvert, she crawls out and stands.

She is alone.

The soldiers have fled, fearing an explosion, and Soon-Ja follows their lead in the opposite direction.

∞

Soon-Ja is forced to camp alone another day while soldiers clear away the wreckage of the Panther jet. She waits another day after they're gone before another convoy passes in the night, followed by soldiers on foot. She follows them and doesn't stop until she reaches the other end of the valley, where she finds a place to camp.

Her spirits soar at the sound of approaching steps until the rational side of her brain takes over and reminds her that Nick moves like a ghost, and she slips into the brush, thankful that she hadn't yet lit a fire.

Soon she hears voices – Chinese voices – and curls up to make herself smaller as one soldier walks towards her. Just before he reaches her, he unbuttons his uniform trousers and begins to urinate. His stream misses her nose by inches. She smells the sweetness of his urine and feels the spray of it hitting her face. It seems to go on forever.

When it stops, he rebuttons his trousers and joins his comrades as they continue on their way.

Moments after their footsteps fade to nothing, another pair of feet appear in front of her, and a hand reaches down to help her stand.

She falls into Nick's arms, trembling.

There are no words that can comfort her. Soon-Ja is emotionally spent.

Nick wraps her in blankets and prepares tea and rice for both. Only then does he remember the chicken tied to his sash. He removes and presents it to her.

things when the soldiers crossed the road after you. I was sure they didn't see you. Luckily, I was kneeling down to put on my A-frame when they crossed, or I wouldn't have seen them."

"Oh."

Soon-Ja seems content with Nick's explanation until she looks at him again.

"What happened to the rest of the chicken?"

Nick taps the pouch on his sash, containing the leftovers.

"I have it right here."

"No, the rest of the chicken. The part you didn't cook."

"That? That was offal. I discarded it."

Soon-Ja mumbles something about Americans' wastefulness as she finishes preparing to leave.

∞

In the nights that follow, Nick and Soon-Ja stumble upon CCP soldiers who appear to have simply lain down and died. They are not the victims of skirmishes like the others they found in days past.

"I'm no pathologist, but I'd say this man suffered from inanition."

Seeing Nick's confusion, Soon-Ja explains.

"Inanition is the severe form of malnutrition or undernutrition."

As she continues to examine him, Nick finds another – one who appears malnourished but has a

48

bullet wound to the back of his head. Soon-Ja confirms that he, too, was suffering from inanition.

"In some cases, inanition causes psychological breaks. This man was likely executed because he was acting psychotic."

"He was disrupting the discipline and good order of the unit?"

Soon-Ja nods.

"I expect we'll be seeing more of this, especially if you're right about their supply channels breaking down."

∞

A few nights later, Nick stops to give Soon-Ja a rest and himself time to think.

"What are you thinking about?"

"Do you see those two mountain peaks silhouetted in the sky?"

Soon-Ja looks in the direction Nick is pointing.

"Yes."

"That's one peak. The gap between them is called a 'saddle'."

"Okay."

"That's due south of us."

Soon-Ja turns back to the road.

"Where is this headed?"

"Right now, it's headed a little south of west."

"When did that happen?"

"The road has been slowly curving for the past mile or so. I suspect that it's detouring around this mountain."

Soon-Ja thinks about Nick's explanation for a moment.

"So, going over that saddle would be a shortcut?"

"Possibly. Probably."

"Are we going to take it?"

"That's what I've been thinking about. There are risks."

"What are they?"

"The path up there and down the other side might leave us stranded."

"And?"

"The weather could turn bad, really bad while we're up there."

"It looks clear. There are lots of stars."

"True, but that can change fast, especially in the mountains."

"And if we keep following the Chinese?"

"We're always taking a risk following them. We never know what we might walk into in the dark."

"Is this what you Americans refer to as 'better the devil you know than the one you don't?'"

Nick chuckles.

"Yes, that's an excellent use of that idiom."

"So which devil will it be?"

"That's for both of us to decide."

Soon-Ja smiles to herself. It's the first time since they met that Nick is treating her as an equal, not just someone unwelcome, tagging along like a little sister.

"I'm inclined to say we take a chance."

"Which chance?"

Soon-Ja points towards the saddle.

"Up there."

"I'm inclined to agree with you. I'll never catch up with the head of this army following them."

"I'm not interested in running towards the fight, but if we simply straggle along as we have been, our luck must run out, and another fight will catch up with us."

"Okay, we're agreed, even if it's for different reasons. Let's start up now until about midnight and then camp. We can go the rest of the way in daylight. It'll be safer, and we can see any bad weather headed our way."

"Okay. I agree."

#

CHAPTER ELEVEN

Storm on the Mountain

As Nick remembers from the topographical map of the Korean Peninsula that he studied, there is no mountain taller than 9,000 feet, and that was much farther north. The saddle they are headed towards may be 7,500 feet. He's certain that they can scale it until a storm rolls in on them when they're about halfway to the summit.

A thousand feet further up, Nick turns when he hears Soon-Ja shout.

"It's a typhoon!"

"It's a gale."

He corrects her, but the wind snatches away his words. Rather than wasting time screaming at one another, Nick takes her hand and resumes marching towards the saddle. Although it's no longer visible, it's a wide enough target that Nick is sure they can't miss it so long as they continue climbing.

Suddenly, the slope falls away, and Nick catches sight of a shadowy object slightly left of their course, and he heads towards it. It proves to be a cabin, and the travelers stagger inside without taking any precautions to ensure that it is safe.

Light filters dimly through one window on the leeward side of the cabin. The other side is packed with wind-blown snow. Although it shines with a spectral glow, there is enough light to search the interior.

Nick fights for almost a quarter hour to close the door. A drift followed them through the doorway, and he must clear it before he can push the door closed and drop the bar in place that Soon-Ja finds leaning against the wall.

When the door is secure, they begin exploring every corner of the cabin and every cabinet and box inside.

Although the cabin walls are stout, the roar of the storm outside forces the couple to shout at each other even when they stand mere feet apart.

They find an iron bed frame with a thick mattress, a small table, two chairs, and kitchen utensils, including a large pot and basin. There is no food, but Soon-Ja shouts triumphantly when she uncovers a stash of salt.

Nick traces the roughhewn logs of the wall with his hand. The gaps are filled with hand-woven cords and dried clay.

"I've seen cabins like this in America but never expected them in Korea."

Soon-Ja was also walking along the walls with Nick, exploring them.

"It's very unusual. Most Korean homes in rural areas are made of mud and wattle."

Nick leaves the wall and picks up a two-gallon can with a handle and a pour spout that he finds in a corner.

"It's full."

After unscrewing the pour spout cap and sniffing, he finds that it is full of kerosene.

Soon-Ja points to a cabinet.

"There's a lantern in there."

Nick also finds a box of wooden matches with the lantern, and soon the cabin is illuminated by a warm glow.

That's when he discovers an iron stove in the center of the one-room cabin. Alongside is a wooden box with kindling and paper, and an iron scuttle full of hard coal. Soon-Ja scoops the pot full of snow that blew through the door as they entered, while Nick starts a fire. In no time, they are dining on tea and rice with the last of the leftover chicken. The chicken and rice are delicious with the addition of the salt that their bodies crave.

After eating, Nick adds more coal, and Soon-Ja is heating more water.

"What's that for?"

Soon-Ja smiles broadly and begins pouring hot water into the basin.

"Bathing."

She adds more snow to the pot, and Nick turns away as she begins to strip. The cabin is now comfortably warm, and she lathers herself with a bar of soap that she found on a shelf under the window.

Nick buries his nose in his Rutter, working on updating his observations until Soon-Ja calls to tell him it's his turn.

When he turns, he finds her under the covers of the bed.

The lather and hot water feel like Nirvana as Nick bathes the upper half of his body. It feels so good that he forgets his modesty and strips off the rest of his clothes to bathe the rest. He is about to redress when Soon-Ja calls him.

"Don't."

Nick turns to find Soon-Ja smiling at him.

"I'll wash our clothes in the morning."

She then lifts the covers, exposing her nakedness, and beckons him to join her.

The sun has set, and the kerosene lamp, its wick lowered to conserve fuel, fills the room with a softer yellow glow as the two lie side by side. Although they are warmer than they have been in months, they don't need each other's body heat. They lie close, facing one another.

Nick opens his mouth to speak, but Soon-Ja places a finger to his lips.

"Don't. There are no words for what we are about to do."

"But..."

Again, Soon-Ja silences him.

"We are of two different worlds. Two different ages. We are different."

"What are we doing?"

"Celebrating."

"What?"

"We're celebrating being alive."

Soon-Ja guides his hand to her breast.

Nick had seen a woman's breast before. He had used his brother's driver's license to sneak into the Gayety Burlesque Theater in Baltimore one night with his friends. Soon-Ja's breasts were nothing like the performers. She had lost all fat during the previous months of privation and exertion. The breasts that Nick had seen in that theater were full; most were sagging. Soon-Ja's are firm. He holds her nipple between his fingers, and it fills and becomes hard. So does he.

Although both are mere students in the art of love, both become teachers.

#

CHAPTER TWELVE

Kimchi and Memories

The storm still rages in the morning while Soon-Ja launders their clothes and hangs them on a rope she strings across the cabin. Nick opens the door twice to retrieve snow for washing and cooking, and fights to close it each time.

They hide under the covers as their clothes dry and speak of small things throughout the day. Shared memories dominate their conversations, and they speak in Korean more and more as Nick's proficiency grows.

Soon-Ja slides from under the covers to turn their garments so that they will dry evenly. Nick follows to tend the fire.

They wrap themselves in blankets to cook tea and rice and return to bed to make love. Their ardor cools as the sun sets. They relight the lantern and cuddle beneath the blankets for warmth.

The couple recollect familiar times and places around the Chesapeake Bay. Scanning the first pages of Nick's Rutter, Soon-Ja studies his sketches of the Little Wicomico River.

"What are these marks?"

Nick rolls from his back to his side to see what she is looking at.

"Those are stakes that the fishermen use to mark the channel."

"Doesn't the Coast Guard take care of that?"

"They can't mark every channel, especially those that shift with every storm and tide."

"So, what good is your drawing. The channel won't be in the same place when you return."

"That's just a reminder of the system they use."

Nick points to a note in the margin of the drawing.

"I spoke to a couple of fishermen at the dock where we moored, and they explained it to me."

Nick flips to the page where he recorded Soon-Ja's observation of the three notches in the trees.

"In addition to the ground-level view as you and I saw it, I made this other drawing speculating on what it might look like from above, as a fighter-bomber pilot might see it."

Back in the early pages describing Nick's trip to Little Wicomico, Soon-Ja sees a sketch of crab traps stacked on a dock next to the fisherman's boat.

"I miss the crabs."

"Please, don't talk about the crabs, not when I'm this hungry for something besides tea and rice."

"I'd settle for kimchi right now."

"What's kimchi?"

"You haven't had any?"

"Did you ever see any in America?"

"No."

"Then how could I have had it? So, what is it?"

A sad smile creeps across Soon-Ja's face.

"It's vegetables pickled with spices and then..."

Soon-Ja pauses as a new expression spreads across her face. One of wonder. Then the dawning realization.

"Then, what?"

"Fermented!"

Soon-Ja leaps from the bed and begins searching the floor of the cabin.

"Fermented in jars and buried in the ground."

"You think there might be some buried here?"

Soon-Ja responds with a huge smile and resumes her search. Nick climbs out of bed, a blanket wrapped around him and begins searching in the opposite direction.

They move slowly, moving the few pieces of furniture, brushing the hard-packed dirt floor with their hands, searching for a telltale clue.

Soon-Ja finds it under the bed. A straight line where the dirt has settled into a crack between the edge of a pit and blanks laid over it, then covered with dirt.

Nick lifts the planks, and Soon-Ja inspects the stash of earthen crocks with wooden lids. As she lifts each lid, the cabin fills with the aroma of garlic, assorted spices, and salt. There are even packets of dried fish!

Soon-Ja prepares a Korean feast using their newfound treasures.

"You like it?"

"I love it!"

"I suppose anything would taste good to you now."

"No, it reminds me of some of the things my mother used to make."

"Like what?"

"Well, she pickled onions and cucumbers in vinegar and sugar."

"And garlic?"

"No, my father hated garlic. He wouldn't allow it in the house."

"Why didn't he like garlic?"

Nick stops chewing and looks lost.

"Nick?"

"It's hard to answer. He doesn't like anything that he associates with people he doesn't like."

"He doesn't like garlic because he doesn't like Koreans?"

"He doesn't like Italians. They use a lot of garlic."

"Why doesn't he like Italians?

"They're Catholics."

"He doesn't like Catholics?"

"Hates them."

"Why?"

"I don't know. I'm not sure he knows."

"Who does he like?"

"Germans."

"Is he German?"

"No. His parents were Slovaks."

"Why does he like Germans?"

"He thinks they're better people."

"He thinks that after what happened there?"

"World War II? He thinks the world would have been a better place if Hitler had won."

"How?"

"I can't tell you. It's his belief, not mine."

They eat without speaking while Soon-Ja digests what Nick has just told her.

"You must be a disappointment to him."

"That I am."

The next time Soon-Ja looks at Nick, she takes his face in her hands.

"Isn't he proud that you became a Ranger?"

Nick ponders the question before responding.

"I don't know. He didn't say."

"Is that why you did?"

"What?"

"Become a Ranger to win his approval?"

Nick chokes on a sardonic laugh.

"No. I wouldn't waste my time."

Nick looks up and sees sadness in Soon-Ja's eyes.

"Don't cry for me. I'm lucky."

"Lucky? How?"

"I have many men I respect who respect me. I have their approval."

"What men?"

"Yachtsmen."

The dinner and their discussion with all of its emotion drain them, and they are soon asleep after Nick cleans up the dishes.

They wake up in the early morning. It's preternaturally quiet. The storm stole away in the middle of the night.

They make love before facing the new day.

CHAPTER THIRTEEN

A Ridge Too Far

Sunlight streams boldly through the cabin window as Nick begins repacking their A-frames, preparing to depart.

"Won't the snow be too deep for us to walk?"

"No. We'll be descending the windward side of the mountain. The snow drifted to the other side."

Soon-Ja masks her disappointment and leaves the bed to help Nick pack. Her forebodings are readily apparent to Nick as they eat their last meal in the cabin. He pulls her towards himself and attempts to raise her spirit by professing his love.

"No, you are running to war, and I am running away from it. Soon we must part, and I'm afraid that neither of us will survive."

"We'll survive."

Soon-Ja sees little hope since North Korea invaded the South. Although she lived among Americans during her education, she never understood their boundless optimism and confidence, which Nick embodies.

"No, no one will survive."

∞

Their final preparation before leaving the cabin is to strap on snow goggles that Nick has carved from wood in the kindling box and strips of cloth torn from a rag.

"The sun will be reflecting from the snow as we descend the mountain. These will keep us from going blind."

"It'll be that bad?"

"Yes, I've experienced the same thing while sailing. I wish I had my sunglasses with me."

They leave the cabin as they found it, less some of the kimchi and dried fish that they take with them. They leave a large portion of rice in exchange.

Their descent progresses swiftly, and they reach a mountain park in less than a day. They are crossing to the far side of the park when they spot a column approaching from the opposite direction.

Nick and Soon-Ja find a vantage point to hide and observe the approaching people. The sight that meets their eyes surprises them. An American GI leads a group of children. Even the smallest of them carries a heavy bundle. The GI carries an old woman sitting astride the A-frame strapped to his back. One hand clutches her collar while the other holds a stick that she uses frequently to beat the GI on his head and shoulders, as well as the backs of his legs. She pours out a stream of hate that not even Soon-Ja can understand.

"What do we do?"

Nick responds by stepping out from hiding and calling out to the GI.

"Where are you going, Corporal?"

The children disappear into the weeds like the tentacles of a sea anemone when touched. The GI pivots towards Nick while dropping to one knee, almost dislodging the old woman on his back, who stares at Nick with abject terror until Soon-Ja steps into view. The old woman then pulls on the GI's hair while shouting and beating him with her stick.

Nick steps forward and takes the stick from the old woman, and she glares at him with unvarnished anger. The GI reaches and takes the stick from Nick and hands it to the old woman, who rewards him with several more whacks about his head. The GI accepts his punishment without complaint.

Nick again takes the stick and repeats his question, and the GI shrugs. His shoulders almost reach his ears because his head is hung low as though beaten down by the old woman's unrelenting blows.

Failing to garner any intelligent response from the soldier, Soon-Ja takes over and addresses the old woman. She speaks to her in Korean, and the woman responds in kind. She then translates for Nick, whose Korean is not yet sufficient to understand the rantings of a crazed peasant woman.

"I asked her where they are going, and she said that she doesn't know. Hell, most likely. She just goes where this... the GI carriers her. She added some pejoratives that I can't translate."

"You don't have to. I can guess."

Nick turns back to the soldier.

"They're going wherever you're headed, Corporal. So where are you headed?"

The soldier responds with a sweep of his hand encompassing the mountains that Nick and Soon-Ja had just descended, then shrugs again.

"There's nothing much that way, and I don't think the children, or the old woman, can survive."

The GI looks up at Nick with a woebegone expression.

"Where should we go?"

It's Nick's turn to shrug.

"Anywhere but there."

The children begin creeping from their hiding places as the minutes pass, and Soon-Ja gently persuades them to gather around. Seeing that they are severely malnourished, she builds a small fire and sends them looking for water. She then boils the water to purify it and cook rice.

Having no plates, she arranges the children and the old woman in a circle and serves a spoonful of rice in their cupped hands. Nick garnishes the rice with bits of dried fish and kimchi.

The first servings disappear long before Nick and Soon-Ja can complete the circuit to deliver the next helping.

After sharing as much as Soon-Ja thinks advisable, she begins examining them.

"We mustn't feed them too much or they'll begin vomiting and won't get any nourishment."

Nick chuckles as the children cling to Soon-Ja like a brood of chicks vying for a favored place near their mother hen. The luckier ones hold Soon-Ja's hands when they aren't ministering to one of the brood, while the others content themselves with clinging to any available scrap of her garments.

Soon-Ja, for her part, appears to enjoy the role.

#

CHAPTER FOURTEEN

Refugees from No Gun Ri

Taking the soldier aside, Nick waves his hand over the entire group – the children and the old woman – who are now gathered around Soon-Ja.

"Where did you find them?"

The soldier mumbles in response, and Soon-Ja translates the question for the old woman.

The old woman spits her response in the direction of the soldier.

"No Gun Ri."

The soldier drops his head into his hands.

Nick leads the soldier aside and sits him down away from the others. He decides to start with a simpler question.

"What's your unit, soldier?"

"Company F, 2nd Battalion, 7th Cavalry Regiment, Sir. The Gary Owens."

"I'm not an officer. I'm just a soldier like you, a private. You outrank me."

"Yes, Sir."

"That's your name, Gary Owens?"

"No, Sir, my name is Hatfield. Tommy Hatfield."

Nick chooses to go gently and ignores the "Sir."

"Who's Gary Owens?"

"We are -- the 7th Cavalry. It's the name of an Irish song. We march to it in every parade."

Nick scans his memory and seems to remember an old John Wayne movie, and the music comes to him.

Tommy looks up at Nick; his head canted to one side.

"You're a soldier? But you're not in uniform."

"I had to pretend to be a Korean peasant to avoid capture."

"You're a spy?"

"No, well... maybe. You could say that."

Tommy smiles briefly until Nick meets his gaze. Tommy quickly looks away, and Nick realizes that he is ashamed of something.

He extends his hand in friendship.

"I'm Nick. Private Nick Andrews."

"And you're a soldier? A U.S. soldier?"

"A Recon Ranger."

Tommy's eyebrows rise.

"That's better than a soldier."

Nick smiles with pride.

"When did you come to Korea?"

Tommy looks up and to the left as he searches his memory.

"It was June, late June."

"Last year?"

"What year is this?"

"1951. January 1951."

"Yes, Sir. Last year. June 1950."

It's apparent now that Nick will have to drag the story out of Tommy bit by bit.

"Where did you come from?"

"West Virginia, Sir."

"That's home?"

"Yes, Sir."

"Where were you stationed?"

"Japan, Sir. The First Cavalry Division in Tokyo, Japan. We were part of the occupation force."

"I thought you said you were with the 7th Cavalry."

"7th Cavalry Regiment, First Cavalry Division."

"What did you do with your unit?"

"Do? We paraded a lot, Sir. There wasn't much to do. We paraded, drank, and whored a lot.

Panic fills Tommy's eyes, and he quickly corrects himself.

"Not me, Sir. I drank, but no whoring!"

"And they sent you to Korea?"

"Yes, Sir. As soon as the North Koreans invaded, General MacArthur sent us. He was our commander and the Governor of Japan. They loaded us on boats, and we got here really quickly. But it was too late."

"Too late for what?"

"They had already driven the South Koreans out of their capitol and almost out of their country. We almost got run down, they were retreatin' so fast."

"What happened then, Tommy?"

"We dug in near this railroad bridge near No Gun Ri. That's a village?"

"Where is it?"

Tommy points aimlessly with a sweep of his arm from East to South to West.

"Somewhere over yonder."

"Then what happened?"

"Refugees come pouring in. The officers told us that they were the enemy dressed like refugees, but..."

"But? But what?"

"There were children and old folks like..."

Here, Tommy points to the group seated with Soon-Ja.

Tommy appears ready to start crying, and Nick gives him time to recover.

"So, you're dug in near where the refugees are sheltering under a railroad bridge?"

"Yes, Sir."

"Yes, Sir. There was a stream and a road alongside, and the bridge over 'em."

"And the refugees sheltering underneath beside the stream and the road?"

"Yes, Sir."

"What happened then?"

"Someone started yelling at us to shoot."

"Shoot at what?"

"At the refugees."

Nick is taken aback.

"Who yelled that?"

"Our lieutenant. I didn't want to, but he threatened me. He got in my face and ordered me to shoot."

"Could you see the enemy?"

"No, Sir. Just the refugees. Children and old folk."

Tommy starts crying again, openly this time.

Nick falls on his back and stares at the sky for several minutes as Tommy cries.

"And you shoot."

"Yes, Sir. I'm a machine-gunner."

"And that's why you allow the old woman to beat you?"

"Yes, Sir."

Nick returns to the old woman and gives back her stick.

#

CHAPTER FIFTEEN

The Recruiter's Crime

Nick is ashamed when he learns that the old woman has already told her the same story – with embellishments -- of the massacre at No Gun Ri.

"How could they?"

"They were poorly trained and poorly led."

"That's an excuse?"

"No, that's an explanation."

Nick wanders back to Tommy.

"Are you gonna turn me in, Sir?"

"Who am I going to turn you into? I don't even know where I am."

"I have a map, Sir."

Nick spins on his heel to face Tommy.

"Why didn't you say something?"

"Uh, you didn' ask, Sir."

"Give it to me!"

Soon-Ja comes to Nick's side when she sees him unfolding the map and laying it flat on the ground. He then turns the map to orient its North to North on his compass.

"He has a map?"

"Yes."

"Do you know where we are?"

"Not yet. The scale is small. It shows a large area, but without the detail I need for accurate navigation."

Half an hour later, he points confidently to a point on the map.

"We're here."

"You're sure?"

"Yes."

Soon-Ja studies the map and the place Nick indicates until she too points.

"I know this area, over here. There's a Catholic mission with a clinic that I visited a couple of times when I started my internship."

Nick studies the location Soon-Ja indicates and the roads in the area.

"It's off the beaten track. It doesn't have any strategic value. I doubt if any military forces are there."

"Should we go there?"

Nick ponders her question before responding.

"Yes, the children need shelter, and this might be a good place."

After explaining the plan to the children and old woman, Soon-Ja places her hand on Tommy's shoulder and speaks softly to him for a few moments. Nick stops her as she leaves the soldier's side.

"Have you forgiven him?"

"Yes."

"Why?"

"He was only following orders."

"Have you heard of the trials at Nuremberg?"

"Yes, why?"

"Every Nazi on trial defended themselves, saying that they were only following orders. The Court's decision was based on a principle of law that military personnel cannot be forced to obey unlawful orders."

Soon-Ja ponders this for a few moments.

"They have to decide for themselves if an order is lawful or unlawful?"

"Yes."

"That sounds like... What do you call it? A trick question."

"Yes, I suppose it is."

"Do you think that someone like Tommy is smart enough to figure it out? Could you?"

Now, it's Nick's turn to ponder.

"That's a fair point. Maybe we should hold his recruiter accountable for putting the gun in Tommy's hands."

Nick avoids responding to the second half of Soon-Ja's question. Thus far, he hasn't had to kill anyone – not directly. Men died when he blew up the boxcar, but that was a consequence of a lawful act of war. Will he be able to make such a sophisticated judgment in the heat of battle? That is a question that will trouble him for a while longer.

Within minutes, everyone gathers their bundles, and Nick leads the march with the children following. Soon-Ja and Tommy follow with the old woman riding Tommy's A-frame, smiting him severely with her stick.

They reach the mission on the evening of the second day after their meeting. Nick goes ahead to scout the location. It appears deserted from a distance, but appearances can be deceiving.

#

CHAPTER SIXTEEN

Ghost in the Chapel

Nick follows a shallow ravine as he approaches the mission in the failing light of day. He studies the small cluster of buildings in the twilight. No smoke betrays a fire. No movement attracts his eye. Even the air is still with anticipation, and the frozen stalks of weeds stand at attention.

Evenly spaced trees in rows on the far side of the mission suggest an orchard, though their limbs are bare in the winter cold. Nick is familiar with apple and pear trees. Maybe these bear the promise of peaches.

He waits for the cover of darkness before crossing the bare ground that separates him from the ravine to the wall of the nearest building, a shed.

One by one, Nick investigates every building. All are deserted. The few pieces of furniture that remain are broken. It appears that refugees or soldiers may have sheltered there, but none recently.

There is no trace of food, but a centrally located well holds the promise of water. Still, the walls are solid, and the windows can be covered to block the winds that make every chill frigid.

Every room in every building has a fireplace, and the kitchen has a large serviceable coal cooktop and oven meant for feeding large numbers of people.

Nick leaves the chapel for last. Surprisingly, the pews remain, though they have been toppled like a row of dominoes. Bibles and hymnals lie scattered on the floor, most well chewed by rodents seeking nesting material. He bends to pick one up when a hand grabs his foot.

"You're out of uniform, Joe."

Nick dives to one side and rises to a fighting crouch with his bayonet in his hand. He is surprised when a nasty-looking, very large blade encircles his neck. His reflexes save him from its edge as he drops and rolls away, again rising in a fighting crotch.

When a voice again sounds behind him, Nick wonders how many are there.

"Very good, Joe. I couldn't have done better myself. My blade has slit many throats, fewer if my victims had been as agile as you."

The voice has the crisp enunciation of someone British, though not a native of the British Isles. Someone from the colonies.

"Who are you?"

A Gurkha infantryman steps out from the shadows in a place that Nick hadn't expected.

"An ally."

"You're a Gurkha."

"Limbu Wotman, at your service."

"How many of you are there?"

"Just me?"

"But..."

Limbu laughs.

"You're good, Joe, but you have much to learn."

Limbu knicks his thumb with the tip of his blade and replaces it in its sheath.

"Who are you, Joe, and why are you leading a band of women and children?"

"That's a long story. Can we get them inside, out of the night air first?"

"Of course."

Nick sheaths his bayonet and accepts Limbu's outstretched hand.

"Nick Andrews. Private First Class."

"Ranger?"

"Yes."

"Young for a Ranger. I'd say, not yet twenty."

Nick glares in response.

"Forgive me, I've never met a young Ranger before. Most are World War II veterans."

"The Army set up a new school."

"Ah, that would explain it. Now let's get those women and children inside."

Nick agrees, and within the hour, they set up the pews and arrange them as beds around a fireplace at one end of the chapel.

Henry gathers firewood from the orchard while Soon-Ja and the old woman inventory the remaining supplies.

Their report settles tomorrow's agenda.

#

CHAPTER SEVENTEEN

The Blood Price

Limbu shares Nick's and his party's breakfast the next morning. He eats with relish but refuses another portion as he observes their depleted supplies.

"You will have to find more soon if you plan on keeping the children fed."

Nick follows his gaze and nods in agreement.

"Have you seen any supply depots nearby that we can raid?"

Limbu's dazzling smile telegraphs his answer.

"Yes, about five miles from here to the east. I've never raided it, so it shouldn't be guarded too well."

Nick nods slowly as he absorbs the information and pulls out the map.

"Tommy?"

Tommy's nowhere to be found.

Soon-Ja looks up from a child's trousers that she's mending.

"He's setting snares for rabbits. He said that he saw some trails on the way here last night."

Nick bends over the map as Limbu points out its location and the best route there.

Nick looks up from the map.

"You'll help us?"

"Of course. My blade hasn't tasted an enemy's blood for a week. That's much too long."

Limbu pulls the blade from its sheath and admires it like a lover. Nick holds out his hands in a gesture asking to hold it, but Limbu shakes his head slowly, indicating no.

"Sorry, PFC Ranger. The hilt is for me. The blade is for my enemy. There is nothing left to share. Forty-seven have satisfied its thirst. Only three more and I'll be a legend."

Nick retracts his hand.

"Sorry."

"There's no need to be sorry. I accept your compliment. Its beauty draws all."

The knife is beautiful in its simplicity. It has no ornamentation. Its form is purpose-made to fulfill its function. The sharp edge is on the inside of the curve of the blade so that when it is drawn across the throat, it easily slits both jugulars in one motion. The sharp blade is backed by a heavy spine so that when it is swung rather than drawn, it will decapitate a victim.

"The point leads the blade when I slash with my kukris. Knives like your bayonet must be thrust to pierce the enemy. Of course, the bayonet is the tip of a spear. Your rifle is the shaft. My kukri is a weapon for the melee, when fighters are too close for spears and swords."

Nick nods his understanding, and Limbu nicks another finger before sheathing his weapon.

Nick's eyes narrow at the gesture.

"Why do you do that?"

"My blade has two rules. It must taste blood every day, and it cannot be returned to its sheath without tasting blood."

Soon-Ja looks up from her chore and shudders.

Nick confers with Limbu about the raid and decides they should leave for the enemy supply depot at noon and arrive there by nightfall. They will take the older children to help carry whatever they steal. Soon-Ja objects until Nick assures her that the children will be kept far from any danger.

"We'll carry the supplies out to them until they can't carry any more. Then we'll take all that we can carry."

Three hours remain before they depart, and Nick uses the time to learn Limbu's story.

Like Nick, Limbu is a straggler, trapped behind enemy lines, although he is in no hurry to rejoin his unit.

"My fight is behind enemy lines. I suppose I could return every morning, but that would waste time. As long as I can forage food, why return?"

"I don't understand. What is your mission while you're behind enemy lines?"

Limbu laughs.

"I kill the enemy. What else would I do?"

"I thought maybe you were sent there to gather intelligence."

"How could I gather 'intelligence' from ignorant Chinese? They don't have any. They are peasants with submachine guns and little or no training other than how to load their weapons and pull the trigger, and run at the enemy."

"What if their weapons jam?"

"Then they use them as clubs. Who knows, the weapons might fix themselves if they hit someone hard enough."

Nick laughs at Limbu's joke until he sees the seriousness in Limbu's eyes. He isn't joking.

"Well, if you're not gathering intelligence, what are you doing?"

"As I said, killing them. They sleep in foxholes, two men, one awake and one asleep. I kill the one awake."

"Why not both?"

"The one asleep will find his comrade dead with a slit throat and realize it could've been him."

"Then what?"

"The one who survives will be alive, but he'll be afraid. His fear will instill fear in others. Maybe they won't sleep. Maybe they'll dissert. Maybe they'll fight among themselves. I kill one, maybe two, ten, or fifty will die. It's very efficient."

Nick nods in agreement.

∞

Tommy returns with a brace of anemic-looking rabbits in time for their noon departure. All of them, including the children, have empty A-frames.

Nick spends the remaining minutes assuring Soon-Ja that he will return with the children the next day. He knows that she will worry and pads his time estimate as much as she'll allow.

His estimate of the time needed to reach the supply depot proves accurate, and they are in position to commence the raid as soon as the Sun sets. Limbu leads the way to dispatch the perimeter guards. Henry remains with the children to supervise them until the way is clear to load up supplies.

Nick is supposed to help Limbu kill the guards but struggles with one while Limbu eliminates the others. The surrounding stacks of supplies muffle the sounds of their fight, and none of the guards on the other side of the depot perimeter are alerted.

Although Nick easily overpowers the enemy soldier, he hesitates to deliver the killing stroke with his bayonet when the man pleads for his life with his eyes. Nick looks up and finds Limbu squatting to one side, watching with a look of disappointment clearly visible, even in the dark. The enemy takes the delay as an opportunity to flip Nick from atop him and reaches for the weapon that Nick had forced from his hand. Limbu's foot prevents him from picking it up. The soldier looks at Limbu in terror, but the Gurkha merely shrugs and does nothing.

Nick tackles the soldier, and their hand-to-hand battle resumes until Limbu grows impatient and steps in to decapitate the man. Nick collapses with the body on top of him and pushes it aside.

Limbu's face is a mask of anger. Nick turns away in shame, but Limbu grabs his shoulder and spins him around.

"Why didn't you kill him?"

"I tried."

"You tried? No, you didn't."

"I would have."

"When?"

Limbu grabs Nick again when he fails to answer and forces him to look at the dead man's face. When Nick turns away, he picks up the head and shoves it face-first in front of Nick.

"See that? That's the look of fear!"

"So what? You said that you killed the enemy to make them fear you."

"Fear is for the living, the ones I allow to live. I owe a quick escape from fear for the ones I choose to kill. Their fear is of no use to me once they are dead. And making someone fear as you kill them is cruel."

Nick hangs his head in shame.

Limbu wipes his Kukris on the dear guard's uniform and sheaths it. He then picks up Nick's bayonet where it had fallen and tosses it to him.

"You've never killed a man, have you?"

Nick shakes his head no and turns away.

"The first one is the hardest."

There is no judgment in Limbu's voice.

"Now, take your bayonet and stab him."

"Who?"

"Him! The dead guard on the ground in front of you."

"Why? He's already dead."

"I know. Stick him. It's called *Blooding the Spear*. It's an ancient tradition among primitive tribes. Even young gang members are taught to kill by blooding the spear. After a fight, they are forced to stab those whom the older gang members killed."

Nick listens, and after several moments' hesitation, he bends forward and pushes his blade into the dead body of the guard.

Limbu growls in disappointment.

"No! Stab him. Stab him with the whole blade. Drive it up to the hilt!"

Nick tries again and again while Limbu eggs him on.

"Harder! Harder!"

Nick's anger grows. If there were daylight, Limbu would see the red rising from Nick's neck to his forehead, until Nick draws back his arm and drives the blade into the dead man to the hilt. Then again. And again.

Minutes pass until the guard's chest looks like ground beef and the fabric of his clothing is inseparable from his flesh.

He continues until Limbu touches his shoulder.

"Enough."

Moments pass while Nick stares at the bloody mess that was once a human being. He drops his knife and holds his hands aloft like a penitent begging forgiveness that the guard can no longer provide.

Nick begins to retch. Falling to one side, he spills his guts onto the ground until he believes that he has coughed up his immortal soul. When it ends, Limbu grasps Nick's shoulder with one hand and uses his other to offer his canteen.

Nick rinses his mouth, then wipes it on the back of his sleeve. He retches again when he discovers blood and bits of body that have stuck there.

More minutes pass until Nick can stand.

"Is that what it's like?"

"No, that was just practice. The real thing is worse, far worse."

"Does it ever get easier?"

"No, unless you're a sociopath."

In time, Nick reaches down and closes the man's eyelids. When he stands, Limbu is staring sternly at him.

"The next time we fight, if you don't kill the enemy quickly and efficiently, I'll kill you myself."

Nick begins to smile until Limbu slaps him, hard, across the face.

"I will. Your failure could get me killed."

Limbu turns to tear a piece of canvas from a stack of supplies and covers the body of the guard, while Nick stares at Limbu's back in shock. When Nick returns to his senses, Limbu looks at Nick.

"Are you ready?"

Nick nods and begins selecting supplies they need as Limbu departs to lead Tommy and the children to the depot.

∞

Limbu returns minutes later with the group, and Nick points out everything he's selected. He continues his inspection as the children load up their A-frames with Tommy's help.

Once the children are packed and ready to go, the three men load up food, coal, and equipment.

He selects a rifle and ammunition for himself and Tommy, but the corporal is too damaged to accept it.

They carry their loot and cache it in a ravine, then return for more. After making sure their raid has not been discovered, they reload and head out.

As they leave, a convoy of trucks approaches the depot, and Limbu returns to see what he can learn while Nick and Tommy lead the children back to the mission.

#

CHAPTER EIGHTEEN

To the Lion's Mouth

Limbu arrives at the mission while Nick and Tommy, helped by the women and children, are sorting through the supplies and storing them. During a short break while the women prepare breakfast, Limbu tells Nick what he's learned.

"The Chinese are massing to attack the Americans at Chip'yong-ni."

"Where's that?"

Limbu unfolds a map that he stole from the supply depot.

"It's here, about fifty miles east of the mission."

"When will they attack?"

"They want to attack as soon as possible, but they're having trouble getting their troops in position. From what they were saying, I'd guess that the attack won't happen until at least a week from now."

"That would give us plenty of time to get there and warn them."

"Don't you think the Americans know about it?"

Nick shrugs.

"Maybe. Maybe not. I don't have very much confidence in our intelligence, not after what I saw at the Yalu River."

"When do you want to leave?"

"We need to get the women and children settled first. I'd say we should be able to leave the day after tomorrow, bright and early."

Limbu agrees, and they decide to begin planning after today's chores are finished.

Nick first needs a uniform, and he approaches Tommy.

"Tommy, will you trade clothes with me?"

Without responding, Tommy begins to strip. He undresses as though he is shedding some part of the guilt he has been carrying since No Gun Ri.

Lucia sees the exchange and takes Tommy's uniform from Nick.

"You'll just have to run around in your underclothes for the rest of the day. These need to be washed."

Nick is not inclined to argue with her.

∞

Nick and Limbu huddle over Henry's map, studying the terrain around Chip'yong-ni and the routes leading to it.

"It seems like a terrible location to defend against a human wave attack?"

Limbu looks at Nick quizzically.

"What does a private know of tactics?"

"I'm not qualified to command a division or a corps, or even a battalion or a company. But every Ranger candidate must lead a tactical exercise."

"Don't officers and senior sergeants attend Ranger School?"

89

"Yes."

"So, you got to lead people who outrank you?"

"Yes."

"I would have paid to see that."

"It had its challenges."

"So, tell me. Why is this such a bad place to defend?"

Nick draws a perimeter connecting all the high ground surrounding Chip'yong-ni.

"How large a force would be needed to defend this?"

"At least a division?"

"Yes."

Nick draws another perimeter around Chip'yong-ni at the base of the hills surrounding it.

"Could you fit the support elements of a division in this area?"

Limbu studies the two perimeters Nick has drawn.

"I think I see what you're seeing. And if a smaller force defends it, they will have to surrender the high ground to the enemy without a fight."

"Exactly."

Limbu studies the map again.

"What if Chip'yong-ni is just a portion of a greater defensive line?"

"What defensive line? It doesn't connect to any terrain that could be considered a place to concentrate forces. No, Chip'yong-ni isn't a salient. It's an outpost."

"Could it be used to stall the Chinese while a larger army is concentrating to engage them?"

"It could be if you're willing to sacrifice those men."

Limbu sits back and releases a sigh.

"I think you're correct. Chip'yong-ni doesn't make any sense unless..."

"Unless what?"

"They don't know what they're facing?"

Nick studies the map again.

"I think you hit the nail on the head."

"They have bad intelligence."

"Yes. We must leave tomorrow to scout the enemy and provide them with better intelligence. Once they know their vulnerability, they can withdraw to a better position."

"And a larger force."

"Yes. They're going to need a larger force."

∞

Nick pulls Soon-Ja aside and tells her that he and Limbu must leave tonight.

"I thought you were going to leave the day after tomorrow. Can't you even wait until tomorrow morning?"

"No, I'm sorry. There might be a massacre if you don't reach the Americans with some vital information before it's too late."

Soon-Ja turns away, sulking.

"Well, if you must, go."

Nick catches Soon-Ja and holds her by her shoulders.

"Please, don't let us part like this."

"Why? We both knew we were going to part."

"I will come back."

Soon-Ja pulls away with determination.

"No, you mustn't. There is no future for us in life or death. Just go. I'll get the uniform for you. It'll probably still be a little damp, but it'll dry while you walk."

Nick waits until she has left the room before turning to gather his few things. Limbu briefly places a hand on Nick's shoulder and then begins preparing to leave.

Nick catches up with Soon-Ja to reconcile with her before he leaves.

"I have to go now."

"I know."

"I don't want to."

"Yes, you do, and I understand. You think you're a coward."

Nick tries to protest, but Soon-Ja puts a hand to his mouth and continues.

"You were afraid of your father. That's reasonable. He is a man to be feared, especially to a young child. You ran away while your platoon was dying. Well, what choice did you have? You were afraid to kill. Yes, Limbu told me. It's not easy to kill, and you still haven't. That doesn't make you a weak man. It doesn't make you a coward. It makes you a good man, and I believe that you'll be able to do what must be done when you have to. Now go. Go to your war, and I'll deal with my guilt."

"What guilt?"

Soon-Ja hesitates only for a moment.

"For surviving."

Nick watches her until she's gone from the room, then turns to go to war.

#

CHAPTER EIGHTEEN

Legend of the Kukri

The mission is about ten miles south of Seoul. Chip'yong-ni is about forty miles northeast of Seoul. Nick and Limbu approach the small rural village by noon the following day after dodging CCP forces concentrating for the attack.

They detour north as far as the single-track railway that enters the village from the west without seeing any end to the enemy lines.

Nick touches Limbu's arm to get his attention.

"We don't have time to scout another route."

"We'll just have to go through them."

"Or..."

Nick thinks while Limbu grows impatient.

"Or what?"

"Someone there has rank and a map."

"Who?"

"Where do we find a general?"

Limbu smiles at the daring of Nick's idea.

"The Chinese have many generals and political officers. They don't have supreme commanders like you Americans or the British. They make decisions by committee. Everyone on the committee will have a map."

"Okay, where do we find a committee?"

Limbu's smile is so brilliant, Nick fears it may give them away.

"You will find a committee somewhere comfortable."

Nick and Limbu assume that the Americans occupy the eight hills that ring Chip'yong-ni and that the Chinese will be massed behind the hills beyond, where they can find cover from observation and attack by American warplanes. Thus, they head for one of the third ring of hills to the west, where they suspect the Chinese command has positioned itself.

They are surprised that the Chinese are drawn up closer than they expect, at the base of the hills surrounding the town. The Americans appear to have abandoned the heights.

"They must have less than a division."

"A battalion?"

"They will be slaughtered. If it's a regiment, they will be slaughtered too. It will just take a little longer."

"We have to warn them so they can get out of there."

∞

Limbu seems to have a sixth sense that helps him find the best route to approach the enemy without being detected. He stops at the base of the hill and turns to Nick to whisper and give him a stern look.

"You must not hesitate this time."

Nick puts all the resolve he can muster into his response.

"I won't."

The two make their way quietly to the closest cover, about twenty yards away from an enemy compound. Starlight provides just enough illumination for Nick to study Limbu's movements as he follows close behind. He imitates them and discovers that he is moving just as stealthily. He is learning valuable skills.

Guards stand in clusters, smoking and talking, their night vision impaired by the flares at the tips of their cigarettes as they inhale. Limbu chooses the group closest to the largest tent and skitters to their side like a land crab. He rises and slashes one's throat in one swift movement, then decapitates the guard standing next to him with another stroke. Their last cries escape their windpipes as gentle sights and clouds of cigarette smoke.

Although Nick follows close behind, Limbu leaves no victims for his bayonet. His purpose is to observe the other guards and watch for any sign of alarm. None is given.

Nick and Limbu separate and sneak a look into the tent from opposite ends like boys at a carnival sideshow. Two kerosene lamps hang from a wire stretched between the tent poles, illuminating a table strewn with maps and papers. Two men stand nearest Nick. A third stands at the opposite end of the table. They are pointing and discussing something in Chinese.

Nick wishes he had taken the other end and that Limbu was at this one, but an alarm sounds before he can duck to the side of the tent to signal his intention. Without hesitation, he spins back to the open tent flap and dives at the two nearest men. He uses his bayonet like a kukri, but it isn't suitable for slashing as effectively as the Gurkha weapon. Although he severs the jugular vein of each man, their windpipes remain intact, and they cry out in their death throes. Nick only has one hand to stifle their screams.

Limbu dispatches the man nearest to him and turns at the sound of footsteps at his end of the tent. Turning back to Nick, he issues a command.

"Grab what you can and go back the way we came. I'll be right behind you."

Limbu has but a fraction of a second to turn back to the open tent flap at his end and meet the sergeant of the guard as he rushes in to die.

Nick grabs maps and documents without looking at them. He hopes he has everything he needs when he turns and runs out into the night. Another guard entering from his end bars the way, but Nick slashes out before he can react. This time, the bayonet takes one jugular and the windpipe.

The light inside the tent fails as Nick races away. Limbu has cut the wire, and the kerosene lamps crash to the ground. Moments later, a brighter light grows as flames leap inside the tent, fueled by spilled kerosene.

Bullets crack overhead as Nick dives into the ravine that he and Limbu had used to infiltrate the camp, followed soon by the thump of the rifles that had fired, telling Nick that his pursuers are close behind. He remembers the path of the ravine well enough to know that he can't outrun the guards' shots in a straight section, so he pauses as soon as he turns a corner and waits for his pursuers. The first guard following runs into Nick's bayonet. The next trips over his comrade's fallen body, and Nick falls on top of him, slashing at his neck. He grabs one of their rifles and runs to the next bend in the ravine as fast as he can. There, he turns and resolves to provide cover for Limbu, who he hopes is close behind.

Even though it is dark, Nick recognizes the weapon as a SKS semi-automatic rifle. The attached bayonet is folded open, ready for use. Good, he thinks, because the magazine only holds ten rounds and one or two might be those already fired at him.

#

CHAPTER NINETEEN

Eyes on Chip'yong-ni

Limbu staggers to the bend in the ravine where Nick waits and falls, his legs weakened from the loss of blood. Three more guards added to the three he killed initially, plus the officer killed in the tent has brought his total to seven for the night. It is only his second-best tally in his career, but still honorable for a Gurkha warrior, and it places his total at more than fifty. He is a legend.

Limbu's smile at the thought turns to surprise when a Chicom soldier pitches back simultaneously with the crack of the bullet that kills him.

"Damn it, Nick, get out of here."

The young Ranger ignores his warning and steps over him. Sighting around the corner, Nick empties his rifle into the darkness, then strips the webbed belt off the soldier beneath his feet and tosses it over his shoulder. A grenade hanging from the belt hits his shoulder, and Nick pulls the pin and tosses it in the direction of the approaching enemies. He then lifts Limbu into a fireman's carry, grabs the fallen soldier's rifle, and takes off running.

Nick runs for two miles before stopping. He places Limbu gently on the ground and discovers blood pumping from his femoral artery. He schools his expression to deny reality but finds Limbu smiling at him when he looks up.

"You are a fine warrior, young Ranger."

He offers his sheathed kukri to Nick.

"You are a fine warrior. You fight like a Gurkha now. You only lack a proper weapon. Take this one."

Limbu shushes Nick when he protests.

"Don't bother burying me. It's not important."

He then pulls his dog tags from the chain around his neck and hands one to Nick.

"Promise me you'll take these back to my family and tell them my story. Return my kukris to them and, if you allow them to adopt you, they will give it back. A kukri must be handed from father to son, and you are my son. They will make it official."

Tears don't come. Not until Limbu makes his dying declaration.

"I am Limbu Wotman, Master Sergeant of the King's Own Rifles."

Limbu dies with dignity. Nick removes the second dog tag from his hand and places in gaps between two upper and two lower teeth. He then presses his palm firmly against Limbu's jaw until the tag is jammed firmly in place.

Nick closes Lumbu's lifeless eyelids and recites a silent prayer. He then strips Limbu's knife belt and loops it over his right shoulder and under his left armpit so that the hilt of the kukri extends above his right shoulder, where he can grasp it quickly in a fight.

Nick travels south for the remainder of the night. He is circling back towards Chip'yong-ni. Morning, he figures, is soon enough to stop and examine what he has taken away.

Two ammunition pouches with forty rounds and a bandage pouch containing cigarettes are attached to the Chinese soldier's web belt. The SKS rifle still has ten unspent rounds in the magazine. Lastly, he pulls Limbu's kukri from its sheath and examines it. Limbu was correct. It feels out of balance until he practices a few slashes with it. The strange blade seems to have a mind of its own and soon adapts to Nick's hand. He chops a two-inch thick branch with one chop. He doesn't feel any hesitation as the weight of the blades carries it through cleanly. A few more slashes, some horizontal and some vertical, complete his training. He can't decide which is the master, him or the blade.

Nick is about to return the blade to its sheath and stops himself. He pauses and then nicks his thumb and squeezes a drop of blood onto the blade. He studies the way the blood spreads evenly along the blade's edge. The capillary effect? He wonders.

With the kukri safely back in its sheath, it is time to study the maps and diagrams. Although the writing is indecipherable, the map symbols are arranged in patterns that he recognizes.

The Americans, it seems, have abandoned any intention of occupying the hilltops surrounding the town as he and Limbu had surmised. The Americans simply don't have sufficient forces to defend a perimeter that would encompass them all. It would take an infantry division to defend Chip'yong-ni properly. The Americans appear to have only a regiment, about one-third the number of troops found in a division.

Normally, a regiment has three battalions. If Nick is interpreting the symbols on the map correctly, this one has four battalions – it is an augmented regiment. One other feature of the map catches Nick's attention. Although he cannot read Chinese, one of the battalions is labeled with Chinese characters that differ from those of the other three. Although he can't understand them, he can see there is something different about the one located on the west side of the perimeter.

The regiment also appears to have a battery of howitzers emplaced just inside the southern sector of the perimeter. He guessed that each battalion has a platoon of heavy mortars, but these and the artillery will be of little use since there won't be any forward observers on the hilltops to direct their fire.

Nick doesn't need to read Chinese documents. The order of battle is simple. Encircle and rush the defenders on all sides simultaneously.

Since Nick has already deciphered the symbols for battalions and companies, he can easily infer that the Chinese outnumber the Americans by at least 12 to 1 if Chinese companies and battalions are similar in size to comparable American units.

The most valuable intelligence that Nick gleans from the maps is the best route for him to follow to avoid the Chinese and approach Chip'yong-ni.

The Chinese also provide detailed drawings of minefield and wire obstacle locations. They lack, of course, the locations of individual mines, providing only the general outline of the mine field.

Nick can read times noted on the maps but not dates. He decides it is safest to assume that the attack will begin after dark today. He has no time to rest. He must be there ahead of the attack to work out a strategy for entering Chip'yong-ni without being killed by the Americans.

#

CHAPTER TWENTY

Flawed Intel

Nick discovers that the Chinese intel is reasonably accurate when he arrives on the high ground west of Chip'yong-ni. For the first time, he sees with his own eyes the railway tunnel to the southeast, one of the few details of the planned attack that he could discern without reading Chinese.

Then Nick spots something the Chinese had not noted on their maps. There's not one but two artillery batteries. The one in the south that they had located is comprised of 155mm howitzers. The other, a 105mm howitzer battery, arrives by road from the east and is also located on the south sector of the perimeter. The alacrity with which the gun crews position their weapons and dig in demonstrates that they expect the fight to begin soon.

However, the deadliest surprise awaiting the Chinese attack and omitted from their maps are ten flak wagons. Each truck mounts a quad-.50 caliber heavy machine guns. The trucks have a capacity of 2.5 tons, which is needed to feed these voracious weapons. These will be able to rip through massed formations of men, mowing them down like grass. Each round they fire has the power to tear apart several human bodies, not just murder them. For the first time, Nick begins to believe that the Americans may not only survive this battle but also win it.

Nick approaches as close as he dares and then waits. It's logical to assume that the Americans will be patrolling all approaches to provide warning of the coming attack. He wants to be found rather than attempting to walk into the town. Crossing a minefield and weaving through wire entanglements is a good way to get yourself killed, especially since he doesn't know the passwords they are using.

Since the Americans are firing mortar rounds onto the hills in preparation for the enemy assault, he remains outside the range of their preplanned final defensive fire. He isn't kept waiting long. A patrol advances cautiously towards him. They are dressed in GI uniforms, and most are carrying M-1 Garand infantry rifles, but their markings are strange to Nick, and they're speaking French.

Nick lays his weapon on the ground and sits with his hand, fingers interlaced, behind his head, facing the approaching soldiers. His heart stops when the point man raises his rifle to fire, but the next man in line reaches forward and depresses the point man's rifle. The shot burrows into the ground halfway between them and Nick.

The patrol spreads out and approaches Nick cautiously. Several men scout the area around Nick to make sure he isn't the bait in a trap. Nick visibly relaxes when their leader speaks to him in English.

"You're American?"

"Yes, sir."

"What are you doing here?"

"Waiting for you to find me."

"Where did you come from?"

"That's a long story, sir. I must talk to your commander as soon as possible."

"*Pourquoi*? Why"

"I have important intelligence to report."

The leader hesitates a few moments to consider Nick's replies and barks an order in French. A sergeant and three soldiers respond by advancing to the front of the line and confer with the leader in hushed tones.

When they finish, the officer turns back to Nick.

"These men will take you to our battalion command post. You will be our prisoner until we can verify your identity. Is that clear?"

"Yes, sir."

The French soldiers pick up Nick's weapons from the ground and frisk him for others. Nick schools himself to avoid reacting when one picks up his kukri. The man's touch on the great knife seems offensive to Nick, as though he and the weapon are now joined as one. They pull the maps and papers from inside his jacket, but don't find his Rutter.

When they are satisfied that he doesn't present a threat, they relax, and Nick is led back along the trail they had followed to reach him while the remainder of the patrol continues its mission.

∞

Nick and his captors follow a long path around the base of the hill until they reach an improved road that leads to Chip'yong-ni. They trot along it past a cut in the hillside where a Pioneer Patrol is embedding fougasses – drums of napalm – and under a railway bridge where they pass through the town's defensive perimeter. Nick is relieved that they are moving quickly. He is certain that they understand that his information is essential.

The guards here are American, and Nick is hopeful that he will be turned over to them, but is disappointed when they continue to the west side of the perimeter, where the French battalion is dug in.

Nick is ordered to sit outside a sandbag-encased bunker with the three soldiers while the sergeant reports inside. The sergeant returns moments later and sits down beside Nick to smoke a cigarette. He offers one to Nick, who refuses. It's a habit he's not yet acquired.

The impact of mortars in another section of the defenses brings them all to their feet. The sound of responding mortars and artillery soon follows. The duel continues for a half hour until a warplane passes low overhead and drops napalm on the far side of the hill north of the town.

The attention of the men assembled outside the French battalion CP is then diverted by the high-pitched whine of a jeep racing towards them. It skids to a halt by the entrance to the bunker where they are seated, and Nick reacts with surprise when a

Lieutenant Colonel who appears older than his grandfather unfolds himself from the seat. He wears a red beret and a bright red scarf as well as a monocle. Nick had heard of such things but had never seen one before. The old man glances around, his eyes hesitating momentarily on Nick, before he grabs a cane and hobbles into the CP, returning everyone's salute.

The sergeant resumes his seat and smokes his cigarette.

"That's our commanding officer."

A few moments later, another officer, a French major exits the CP and approaches Nick.

Nick snaps to attention and reports.

"Private First-Class Nicolas Andrews, First Ranger Battalion, First Recon Ranger Platoon, reports, sir."

The Major returns his salute.

"Major Claude Moreau, Ranger. Follow me inside."

Major Moreau dismisses the sergeant and his men to rejoin their unit and leads the way into the CP. It takes several moments for Nick's eyes to adjust to the dark. The battalion commander and his staff gather around a wooden field table, examining Nick's maps and documents.

The French officers speak in hurried tones for several minutes while Nick waits at parade rest beside Major Moreau until the battalion commander looks in their direction.

"This is the man who brought these?"

#

CHAPTER TWENTY-ONE

A Day Late

Major Moreau introduces Nick to the French commander and his staff.

"This is Private First-Class Nicolas Andrews, Ranger, U.S. Army."

He then turns to Nick to formally introduce his commander.

"Private Andrews. Lieutenant Colonel Manclar, commanding."

The old man eyes Nick through his monocle for several moments, its lanyard swinging gently whenever he moves his head.

"Where did you get these?"

"We stole them from a Chicom command tend about two miles west of here, sir."

"We?"

"Yes, sir. A Gurka Master Sergeant, Limbu Wotman, and I."

"Where is Master Sergeant Wotman?"

"Dead, sir.

Nick pauses to swallow his emotions.

"I had to leave his body."

The French colonel nods his understanding, then turns his attention back to the documents.

"Do you read Chinese, Private?"

"No, sir. But I can read maps, and I've seen your defenses as they've seen them, and I've seen their preparations."

The colonel looks up at Nick appraisingly.

"We don't read Chinese either; however, like you, we can read maps, though we haven't seen what you've seen."

Colonel Manclar twitches his fingers, and an aide brings him a camp stool. When the colonel is seated, he asks Nick to explain what he's seen.

"I suspect you've seen much, Private, and I hope to live to hear your story. However, the Sun will soon set, and this battle will commence. Tell us what you've seen in, say, the past forty-eight hours. No opinions, just facts."

"If I may be permitted one observation outside your limit. I've been travelling with a doctor for the past couple of months and she..."

"She?"

"A young Korean intern, educated in the United States."

"Where is she?"

"Safely tucked away in an abandoned mission about 50 miles southwest of here, and well provisioned."

"Where did the provisions come from?"

"We stole them from a Chicom supply depot."

"We, being you and the Gurkha?"

"Yes, sir."

"Continue."

"The doctor examined some dead CCP soldiers we found, and she is convinced that they died of inanition."

Colonel Monclar glances over his shoulder at another officer wearing a caduceus on his collar.

"Inanition is death by malnutrition, sir."

Monclar nods his understanding.

"Continue."

"I felt I should mention this because it concerns the state of the enemy you are facing."

"Thank you, it was a wise point. Continue."

"We, Sergeant Limbu and I, approached Chip'yong-ni from the southwest..."

"From the mission?"

"Yes, sir. We had studied the town earlier on another map and guessed that it was likely surrounded. We decided to raid a command center to obtain one of their maps so that we could determine the best way to slip past them."

"You chose to enter a surrounded town? For what purpose?"

"To deliver intelligence that I have been gathering ever since I parachuted onto the Yalu flood plain."

"You came here from the Yalu River? How?"

"Walked, sir."

"When did you start?"

"We parachuted the night that the CCP army crossed the Yalu."

"We? You and the Gurkha?"

"No, sir. I met him later, at the mission. I parachuted with a Recon Ranger platoon."

"Where are the rest of your platoon?"

"Dead, sir. All dead. We landed on top of the Chinese. I'm the only survivor."

Colonel Monclar looks at Nick with something else in his eyes. Sympathy? Respect?

"Continue."

"I was bringing this."

Here, Nick reaches inside his jacket and produces his Rutter.

"What is this?"

"It's my observations from the Yalu to here. It contains sightings that can be used to recreate my route and locate CCP supply depots and ammunition dumps as well as bivouacs where they rest during the day."

Another staff member in the back and reaches past the colonel. Colonel Monclar nods to Nick.

"Please allow him to look. He's my G2 – Chief of Intelligence. Now, please continue, but limit your observations to the most recent deployments of the Chinese."

"Yes, sir. I can only speak to those north and west of your defensive perimeter. They were drawn up close to the base of the hills 12 hours ago when I last saw them. Although they weren't moving at that time, I suspect they are moving towards the crest of the hills as we speak."

"So that they will be in position to launch their attack after the Sun sets."

"Yes, sir."

"What about artillery and tanks?"

"Very little, sir. Some small-bore howitzers and no tanks. Plenty of mortars."

"Do you have an estimate of their numbers?"

Nick hesitates. The colonel wanted observable facts. Now he's asking for an estimate, and that's all Nick can offer.

"Based on my interpretation of their map, I estimate that you are outnumbered twelve to one."

A murmur passes among the assembled staff arrayed behind the colonel, and he raises his hand to quiet them.

"That is significantly greater than our estimate."

"Sorry, sir."

"No, I suspect that your estimate is based on better input than ours. If we had known this a few days ago, we likely would have withdrawn."

"That is not likely possible now, sir."

"No, it is not."

The colonel's mind is awash with many concerns, all exacerbated by the intelligence that Nick has just delivered. Still, a new thought intrudes on his deliberations.

"Was there anyone in this tent when you and the Gurkha stole the map and documents?"

"Yes, sir. A general, a civilian, and a guard."

'What happened to them? We entered the tent from opposite ends. The guard was closest to Sergeant Limbu."

"And the other two?"

"I was closest to them."

"Both dead."

"Yes, sir."

The colonel smiles with new respect and consults his watch, then hobbles to the door of the bunker with the aid of his cane. After several minutes, he returns and takes Nick's Rutter from his G2's hands.

"Is this as valuable as I think it is?"

The G2 nods.

"Most assuredly, sir."

The colonel waves his aide forward and hands him the Rutter.

"Deliver this to Colonel Freeman immediately."

Colonel Monclar turns to Nick and instructs him to follow his aide but is cut short when mortar rounds begin to fall.

"Too late, take Private Andrews to my quarters and place his Rutter in my document stash box."

The colonel begins to turn away.

"Wait! Private Andrews, I need you to help my battalion artillery officer determine where those damn mortars might be. My aide will hide your Rutter in a safe place in my tent. It's an ammo can buried under my footlocker. If you survive this battle, you'll find it easily enough. If you don't, someone – hopefully one of us – will find it."

The colonel then turns to his assembled staff.

"You have your duties. Carry on, and God have mercy on all of us."

Nick adds a salute that he learned from one of the World War II veterans in his Recon Platoon.

"For what we are about to receive, let us be grateful."

The staff responds with shock, followed by a laugh, and join in like a chorus in a Greek tragedy.

"Amen."

#

CHAPTER TWENTY-TWO

The First Blow

The Chinese map does not use the same grid system as American maps, so Nick first contacts the fire control center to establish a compatible system by comparing the locations of known geographic features common to both their map and the one he stole. Using this system, he can plot artillery and mortar locations from the Chinese map onto the American map.

The French artillery officer relays coordinates to the 105mm and 155mm howitzer fire control center as Nick reads them from the Chinese map and converts them to grid references that the American artillerymen can use.

When the task is complete, Nick exits the bunker to greet a new world, not yet completely dark. The sides of the hills, once barren, are now flooded by a swarming mass. Its individual members aren't discernible in the half-light, nor are the individual sounds of men in motion. It is a muffled roar of men venting their fear in warlike cries punctuated by the blaring of bugles and the shrill commands relayed by whistles like cops attempting to sort out a traffic jam.

As the mass descends on the French defensive line, a new sound is heard. It starts out soft, unrecognizable. Slowly it grows in volume, a wailing sound, a kind of siren. It's a hand-cranked air raid siren that the French found somewhere in the guts of the town. The wailing reaches its apogee and then fades slightly. In a moment, it resumes its climb in volume, and the piercing tone almost becomes painful.

The siren is a signal, and Nick witnesses a new sight – an improbable sight. The French begin emerging from their foxholes with bayonets fixed to the muzzles of their rifles. They are charging. The few are charging the many, and the many stop, turn, and flee.

Other French infantrymen – Nick assumes sergeants and junior officers – begin rounding up their subordinates and coaxing them back into their foxholes.

It's not a victory.

It's a promise of victory against impossible odds if the defenders have the will and courage to make it happen.

∞

Nick returns to the French Battalion CP, seeking a place for himself in this battle. The kukri on his back seems to be egging him on.

He finds Major Moreau tagging along behind Colonel Monclar, who is hobbling back and forth on his cane behind the front line of foxholes where a human wave is being held at bay by the grit of Foreign Legionnaires decimating the ill reputation earned by French forces during World War II, backed up by the firepower of a flak wagon.

One foxhole is overpowered and overrun, allowing a ripple of the human wave to break through and head directly at Colonel Monclar, who defends himself with his cane and a revolver.

Just as he and his adjutant are surrounded and about to succumb to the tidal forces of the attack, a new force arrives, a slashing blade that rips at the necks of Chinese soldiers, decapitating many.

Nick's kukri joins the battle.

#

CHAPTER TWENTY-THREE

Forgotten Memories

The room is white. People chatter quietly in the distance, and the aroma of antiseptic wafts in the air. A bird song interrupts the stillness intermittently.

Nick is confused. His eyelids thwart every attempt to open them, and his lips feel parched and won't open. His tongue refuses to obey his commands any more than his eyelids. Bedsheets cool and starched rest on his body.

He wonders.

"What fool would starch bedsheets?"

He can feel his arms and legs, feet and hands, but all are beyond his ability to control.

Time passes unmeasured. Someone comes and goes periodically, bathing him or slipping an ice chip into his mouth. On several occasions, a voice with a commanding quality speaks nearby, asking questions that more subservient voices attempt to answer. Nick recognizes the language but few of the words.

Slowly, after many attempts, Nick's eyelids flutter open and then close immediately against the glare of light first seen.

He doesn't try again until he has better control and can open them narrowly to filter the light until his eyes become accustomed.

His first sight is rewarded with the vision of a pretty, young woman hovering over him. She's dressed in white, and he believes that she is an angel suffused in a heavenly glow. Over time, her features become more matronly, but her smile remains beautiful. She speaks softly with a note that seems to welcome Nick back to the land of the living.

"Good evening, Ranger."

Nick wants to remark on her beauty, to profess his love. Other words emerge from his mouth in a dry croak.

"Where am I?"

"You're in a hospital in Tokyo."

"Tok...?"

"Tokyo, Japan."

Nick tries to nod, belches.

"Forgive..."

The nurse chuckles.

"Rest now. I'll tell the doctor that you're awake."

"What happened?"

The nurse's smile is replaced by a look of concern that shows in her eyes.

"You don't remember?"

"No."

"Anything?"

"Nothing."

She straightens his covers and pats them in place.

"Don't worry. It'll all come back when you're ready. Rest now."

"But I was home."

"You were dreaming."

"It was a nightmare."

"In Korea?"

"No. Home."

Nick doesn't have the strength to complete the conversation.

A succession of doctors and nurses tend to Nick for another week as he drifts in and out of consciousness. He mourns the loss of numbness as he becomes aware of the stabbing aches and pains that afflict every square inch of his body. Even the hair on his head seems to hurt. The nurses provide painkillers judiciously.

"We don't want you to become addicted."

Another week passes before Nick can move his head. He rolls it from side to side to survey his surroundings. Unfortunately, his eyes fail to focus on anything beyond a few inches.

Something pinned to his pillowcase annoys him when he rolls his head to the left. He can't make out what it is. The morning nurse tugs at the pillowcase and brings two medals pinned to it into view: a Silver Star and a Purple Heart.

"Whose are those?"

A giggle accompanies the nurse's response.

"Yours, silly."

"Mine?"

"Both yours."

"What are they for?"

"Well, the Purple Heart is obvious. You've been wounded. You should have a whole footlocker full of Purple Hearts. You had 52 stab and bullet wounds requiring surgery, but they only give one per incident."

"I was wounded more than once?"

"Many more. You don't receive Purple Hearts for the concussions and broken bones."

"How bad were they?"

"The doctor will review them with you."

"The Silver Star?"

The nurse leans forward and places a gentle hand on his cheek.

"You're a hero."

"A hero? What did I do?"

"Don't you remember?"

Nick struggles, but his mind won't go there. He only finds blackness where a memory should be.

"No."

"Don't worry about it. That's normal. Someone will talk to you later."

∞

The doctor sits next to Nick's bed, with a clipboard on his lap, a pen in his hand.

"The nurse says you were having nightmares."

"Yes, when I first woke up."

"You say you can't remember the battle at Chip'yong-ni. Did the nightmares help?"

"The nightmare had nothing to do with Korea."

123

"What was it about?"

"Home?"

"What about home?"

"My pop."

"Was someone hurting him?"

Nick laughs. Not a funny laugh.

"No one ever hurt my pop."

"Why?"

"He was a prizefighter."

"I'm sure he was hurt in the ring."

"Maybe. I don't know. He stopped fighting, prize fighting, before I was born. My brother remembers."

"He's older than you?"

"Yes, more than six years older."

"Why did he stop?"

"I don't know."

"Did he lose a lot?"

"No. They tell me he always won."

"But he wasn't the one hurting in the nightmare."

"No. He was hurting me. My brother. Mom."

"How was he hurting you?"

"With his fists."

The doctor pauses to make notes.

"I'm surprised that you haven't been dreaming about the war. It must've been far more brutal than your father's abuse."

"No."

"Why?"

"I expect the enemy to hurt me."

"Did you ever hurt the enemy?"

"Yes, a couple of times."

The doctor refers to a paper on his clipboard.

"Just a couple of times?"

"I had never killed anyone before..."

"Before what?"

"Limbu and I raided a supply depot, and I couldn't kill a guard."

"Limbu?"

"A Gurkha sergeant I hooked up with. He said I would get him killed if he couldn't trust me."

"Trust you? For what?"

"To help him kill the enemy."

"This made him angry?"

"Yes, sir. A soldier must do his part, or his buddies will have to fight their share and yours."

"I see. What did Limbu do?"

"He taught me to kill?"

"How?"

"He had me blood my spear."

The doctor nods slowly, knowingly.

"I've heard of that. And then you could kill."

"Yes."

"How many?"

"Two with a knife. A couple more with grenades and rifle fire."

The doctor checks another paper on his clipboard.

"That's maybe a half dozen?"

"I suppose, sir."

The doctor takes a sheet of paper from his clipboard and hesitantly hands it to Nick.

"I'm not sure I should show you this, but you must face reality sometime. Maybe now is as good a time as any. It's an outline summary of many statements taken from witnesses of your actions at Chip'yong-ni."

Nick reads.

"Statement of Major Claude Moreau, French Foreign Legion, Adjutant – 'Lieutenant Colonel Monclar and I were being rushed by a group of approximately ten CCP soldiers who had broken through our defensive perimeter when Private First-Class Nicolas Andrews threw himself into their path and, despite being shot and stabbed several times, decapitated all ten in a matter of seconds.'

"Statement of Lieutenant Henri Bordain, French Foreign Legion, Aide to Colonel Monclar – 'I was knocked off my feet by a rifle butt thrust to my chest by a CCP soldier. I witnessed Private Andrews leap over me and decapitate every member of a group of CCP soldiers who had broken through our defensive perimeter.'

"Statement of Sergeant Paul Gordon, French Foreign Legion, Squad Leader – 'The battle of Chip'yong-ni progressed all night, and just about dawn, everyone on both sides was exhausted. Ammunition was totally expended, or weapons had been rendered inoperable. Hand-to-hand combat among widely separated groups continued. I witnessed Private Andrews, propped up by a pile of bodies of the enemies he had killed, fighting with the blade of an entrenching tool in his left hand that he used like a shield and his knife in his right hand. The enemy seemed drawn to him. He had been shot and stabbed countless times and continued killing them, most by decapitation or with neck wounds.'

"Statement of Sergeant Harry Wilkins, U.S. Army, Graves Registration – 'I have never seen anything like it, so many men killed by decapitation. Most were located surrounding Private Nicolas Andrews. Witnesses reported that he had killed them all during the fighting that lasted all night. We counted sixty-two killed by decapitation and numerous others by neck wounds by knife.'"

The doctor takes the summary from Nick's hand and replaces it on his clipboard.

"Does that help you remember anything?"

"No, sir."

"And you haven't dreamed of anything like it?"

"No, sir."

The doctor flips to the last page on his clipboard.

"Just one last question for today."

"Sir?"

"The nurses report that you repeatedly reach behind your head with your right hand in your sleep as though expecting to find something there, and that you murmur something unintelligible as you do this. Do you have any idea what this may be?"

Nick ponders the question for several minutes and then lies.

"No, sir."

CHAPTER TWENTY-FOUR

Attention to Orders

Two weeks after his visit with the Army psychiatrist and many other doctors, Nick is visited by the Commander of the United Nations Command, Korea, General Matthew Ridgeway, accompanied by his aides and adjutant. A French officer wearing the gold oakleaf of a major is there in a wheelchair with his leg in a cast and his arm in a sling. Nick thinks that he recognizes him, but isn't sure.

"You were there."

"Yes. Major Moreau."

Nick is relieved that he hasn't lost his mind. The battle was real, and he remembers the events leading up to the Chinese breach of the French defenses, though he still has no memory of what came after.

The general smiles at Nick as a father should have, or as his surrogate fathers had.

"How are you doing, son?"

Nick struggles to sit up, but a doctor restrains him.

"No need for formalities yet. I'm sure the general won't mind."

"No, I don't expect you to be up and ready for another fight, not yet."

All around chuckle, except Nick.

"I'm getting better, general. I must be. That's what the doctors and nurses keep telling me."

All chuckle again with less enthusiasm.

"Are you up for a little business?"

"Yes, sir."

"Good, I see you have your Purple Heart and Silver Star. You Division Command General awarded those."

"Yes, sir. What are they for?"

The general smiles but ignores Nick's question.

"Major Moreau has more time to spend with you than I, and he has firsthand knowledge. Adjutant!"

A colonel steps forward with orders in hand.

"Attention to orders!

General Order 48.

In recognition of his outstandingly meritorious service and achievements in service to the unified command of the United Nations Forces in Korea, Private First-Class Nicolas James Andrews, Recon Ranger, is hereby promoted to the rank of Second Lieutenant, United States Army Reserve.

By order of the Commander

Matthew B. Ridgeway

General, United States Army

For the Commanding General

Harry Pendergast

Colonel, United States Army

Effective this date

Congratulations, Lieutenant."

General Ridgeway pins the shiny gold bar to Nick's pillow above his Silver Star and Purple Heart.

"Congratulations, Lieutenant. And that's not all. Adjutant."

Again, the colonel steps forward with a new set of orders.

"Attention to orders!

General Order 48.

On the night of 14 October 1950, then Private First-Class Andrews parachuted onto the Yalu River flood plain between North Korea and the People's Republic of China, together with the other members of his Reconnaissance Platoon, to ascertain enemy dispositions and intentions. Landing on the enemy forces as they crossed the Yalu River, all members of that platoon except Private Andrews were killed. As the sole survivor of that incident, Private Andrews embarked on a march of exfiltration of approximately 350 miles through enemy territory until reaching Chip'yong-ni on 13 February 1951, where he voluntarily fought alongside French allies in the defeat of a numerically superior CCP army. Along the way, he recorded countless observations that have enabled United Nations forces to locate strategic enemy supply depots, ammunition and fuel dumps, and bivouac areas, all camouflaged to avoid detection by aerial reconnaissance. The destruction of these locations has significantly reduced enemy effectiveness and diminished their ability to wage war. His accomplishments have exceeded those of any other intelligence-gathering effort in the annals of war.

In recognition of his outstandingly meritorious service and bravery in service to the unified command of the United Nations Forces in Korea,

Second Lieutenant Nicolas James Andrews, Recon Ranger, is hereby awarded the Distinguished Service Cross.

By order of the Commander
Matthew B. Ridgeway
General, United States Army
For the Commanding General
Harry Pendergast
Colonel, United States Army
Effective this date
Congratulations, Lieutenant."

General Ridgeway pins the Distinguished Service Cross to Nick's pillow to the left of his Silver Star and Purple Heart.

"Congratulations, Lieutenant. That's from me. The President may have another for you soon. You've been recommended for the Medal of Honor for your actions in the battle at Chip'yong-ni. Honestly, you are worth a division of infantry to me and this war effort. Thank you, Lieutenant."

∞

All leave except Major Moreau.

"I also have something for you."

Moreau pulls aside a lap robe, revealing Nick's kukri in his sheath.

Nick grabs the knife and holds it close as though he had caught the Major attempting to steal it. Moments later, he begs the Major's forgiveness.

"Don't worry, I understand."

Nick begins to withdraw the blade from its sheath, but the Major stops him.

"Don't! I don't think your body can afford to lose any more blood right now."

#

CHAPTER TWENTY-FIVE

The Gettysburg of Korea

Major Moreau is assigned the bed next to Nick's, and they convalesce together for the next few weeks. He tells Nick the events at the battle of Chip'yong-ni at the request of doctors who hope it will help restore Nick's memory.

"You remember nothing?"

"Not a thing. Can you tell me?"

"We had a bit of a reprieve after our men broke the first assault. The second assault came later, and I don't know how many of the enemy were cut down by the flak wagons or the rifle and machine gun fire from our positions. Wave after wave of them came at us. The ones behind pushed those ahead, each rank dying in its turn."

Major Moreau pauses to take a drink of water while Nick waits. None of this sounds familiar to him.

"You wouldn't have seen the first hour or two because you were helping plot fire orders for our artillery and mortars. I remember a glimpse of you arriving when a rank of Chinese soldiers reached our foxholes. The colonel and I were right behind our men, plugging up the gaps with our reserves. Then there were no reserves, and the Chinese began squeezing through the gaps. Ammunition was running out, and weapons with ammunition were beginning to misfire. The men were fighting hand to hand – rifle butts, bayonets, knives, fists, rocks, anything at hand."

Nick is breathing heavily and turns away.

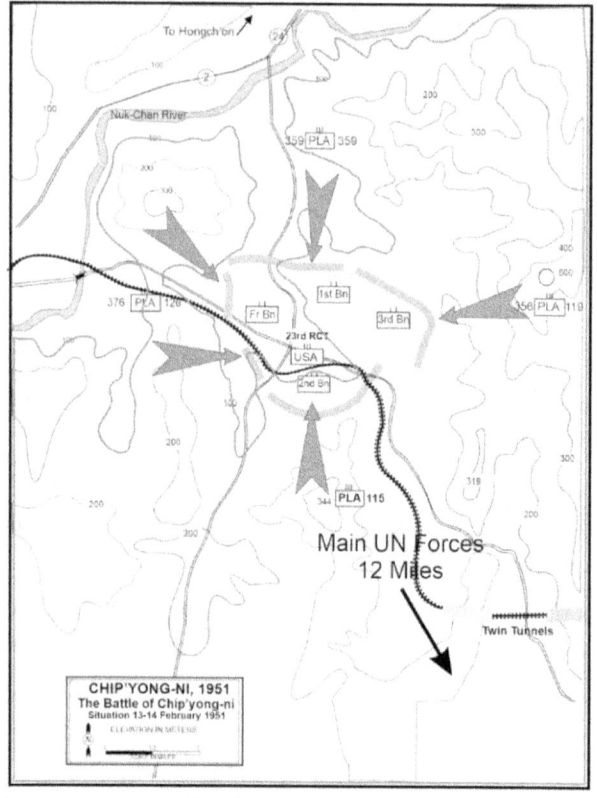

"Are you remembering?"

"No."

"Why did you turn away?"

"I'm ashamed that I can't remember."

Moreau puts a hand on Nick's shoulder.

"You have nothing to be ashamed of. This is where you arrived. Colonel Monclar and I were surrounded, and we were dead."

Nick is leaning forward now, his eyes bulging.

"Then heads began disappearing. The Chinese were dropping headless to the ground as you tossed their heads aside. I've never seen or heard anything like it. One stroke, another head. The colonel and I were forgotten. Every Chinese soldier turned on you. Those whose guns still fired shot you. Those who couldn't, stabbed you. The rest beat you with rifle butts, sticks, rocks, fists. At times, you were lost to sight in the melee, only to reappear as one rank after another fell like wheat being harvested."

Nick sits down hard.

"Are you okay?"

"Yes."

"You just fell."

"How long did I keep killing?"

"Honestly, I don't know. It might have been minutes or hours. Time lost all meaning."

"How long did the battle last?"

"All night. The Chinese began withdrawing when dawn broke."

"Why didn't they withdraw earlier? They needed time to reach their fallback positions before the warplanes arrived."

"That's the thing. They didn't. They started to withdraw until their sergeants blew their whistles. They must have been ordered to reengage because that's what they did."

"They stayed in the open when the Sun came up?"

"Yes. That's why they lost. Our warplanes bombed and strafed the hell out of them."

"That doesn't make sense."

Major Moreau nods in agreement.

"The best we can agree on is that they were close to winning and didn't want to give up what they had gained. They had overrun the 155 howitzers. The cannoneers spiked their guns before withdrawing. The gun crews on the 105 howitzers pulled their pieces away by hand and retreated with the infantry to their fallback positions."

Both men sit quietly for many minutes, gathering strength to continue.

"And that was the end of it?"

"No, they reengaged the next night, after the Sun had set and the planes were gone. There weren't nearly as many of them, and their attack only lasted an hour or two."

Nick struggles to fit the Major's narrative into a memory but can't find one.

"How long did I last?"

"You almost made it to sunrise that first night. When I saw you the next morning, you were propped up against a pile of your victims with your head bent forward at an impossible angle. Everyone thought you were dead. You were left for Graves Registration until a passing medic noticed air bubbles emerging from a chest wound. That's when you were evacuated to a field hospital."

Nick begins shaking.

"What's happening? Should I call a doctor?"

"No."

"Why are you shaking?"

"I'm afraid."

Moreau tips his head to one side, looking at Nick in wonder.

"Afraid? Afraid of what?"

"I've lost my mind."

Nick and the Major walk slowly back to their ward without speaking. They don't talk again until they awaken from naps.

"Maybe it's best if I never remember."

"No. You must remember."

"Why?"

Moreau hesitates to respond.

"It's a battle worth remembering."

"Why? It's just another battle."

"It's significant. They're calling it the *Gettysburg of Korea*. I didn't understand until I read the history of your Civil War, and many comparable elements make Gettysburg an apt metaphor for what happened at Chip'yong-ni."

Nick decides to help the Major by explaining his reasoning.

"I've studied Gettysburg and think I see what they're talking about. Obviously, we won."

"Yes, we did, decisively."

"Okay. Before Gettysburg, the Confederate States of America had won the most significant battles. They won them with generals like Stonewall Jackson, who was a master of battlefield maneuver. He always showed up when and where least expected. Lee's thrust into the North was intended to cause the Union to sue for peace. It didn't work. He was forced to sneak back into Virginia severely wounded. Thereafter, the war wound down."

"From your lips to God's ears, I hope this one will wind down as well."

∞

Over the weeks that follow, Moreau teaches Nick to speak French. The younger man not only heals faster but also learns faster, as Moreau begins by teaching him the rules of French reading. Nick is surprised that he can easily recognize about a third of each book that the Major gives to him.

"Many say that English is French badly spoken."

"I can't argue. I can now read the words correctly and, even though they are spelled differently, I can see the similarity to their English counterparts when I sound them out."

Nick also quickly picks up French Grammar, but Moreau warns him.

"One of the hardest parts in learning any language is its idiom. Look at your own language. British and American English speakers frequently have trouble conversing because their idioms are so different."

"Would it also follow that you have trouble conversing with a French-Canadian?"

"Absolutely."

Nick's French lessons continue as their convalescence allows them to walk outdoors.

"I really appreciate the lessons in French. I might've lost my mind from boredom if we hadn't done this."

"Yes, time has passed more quickly for me also, but to be honest, I must admit I had another reason."

Nick waits expectantly.

"You will have reason to travel to France soon, and I will accompany you."

"Why?"

"You have been awarded the Croix de Guerre, one of France's highest awards for valor."

Nick turns away. He is conflicted at the news.

"What is the matter, my friend?"

"I can't accept that."

"Why not?"

"I wasn't brave."

"Of course you were. I witnessed your bravery."

"What is bravery?"

"That's a very philosophical question."

"Not for me. I've been pondering it recently. The dictionary tells me that bravery is fearlessness. I think that's wrong. To me, fearlessness is foolishness."

Moreau laughs softly and then stops himself.

"I can see the sense in what you say. How do you Americans say 'Only fools rush in.'"

"Exactly."

"So, what is your definition of bravery?"

"The best I can come up with so far is 'acting despite fear.'"

Moreau considers Nick's definition carefully.

"I like that. It sounds right. For those of us who have faced our fears on the battlefield, you make a lot of sense."

"Okay, now look at it from my point of view. Yes, I acted bravely, but I felt no fear. I've been talking to the doctor, and he told me about a dissociative fugue state. He says it's a kind of reversible amnesia. A person may act without remembering it or even being aware of it. Since I can't yet remember the events at the battle, mine may not be the reversible amnesia."

"In other words, you were simply acting without being aware."

"Right! And if I wasn't aware, there was no fear."

"And if there is no fear?"

"There is no valor."

"It seems to me that you are judging yourself very harshly."

"I'd rather be harsh with myself than have to return your award when you figure out, I was more like a drunk soldier than a brave one."

Moreau laughs but stops when he sees that Nick isn't.

"You're serious?"

"Yes."

#

CHAPTER TWENTY-SIX

The President's Request

Nick sits in the reception room outside the Oval Office as a steady stream of military liaisons and civilian aides, as well as an occasional member of Congress, form a steady stream of traffic, meeting with the President. He picks nervously at the new lieutenant's uniform, which he purchased with a loan from his brother. Nick had entered the Army with little savings and had earned enough as an enlisted man to afford the new uniform. He thought of having his mother sew stripes on the trousers and around each jacket cuff, but she insisted that he needed a proper uniform to meet the President.

Truman stands and walks to meet Nick as he is welcomed into the President's office. A photographer snaps the obligatory shots for a press release before the President dismisses everyone except Nick. Truman invites Nick to sit in a comfortable wingback chair near the fireplace as he pours a shot of bourbon into each of two crystal neat glasses and offers one to Nick, who holds up a hand.

"No, thank you, sir."

"A soldier who doesn't drink?"

Nick blushes.

"I'm not old enough, Mr. President."

The President thrusts the glass into Nick's hands.

"You're old enough to bleed for your country, you're old enough to drink."

Nick accepts, and they drink in companionable silence.

Nick sips and almost chokes on a laugh.

Truman looks at him with a question in his eyes.

Nick wipes his mouth with his hand and explains.

"I just thought that now I know why it's called 'firewater'. The joke made me start to laugh before I could swallow it."

The President smiles and chuckles.

"Yes, that's an accurate observation. Funny, too."

Truman returns to the sideboard to refill their glasses from a matching crystal decanter and sits in the chair opposite Nick after delivering his.

"Now, what's this business I hear about you refusing to accept the Medal of Honor, son? And you've refused the Croix de Guerre? The French rarely offer that trinket to anyone but their own."

Nick explains his reasoning as he had discussed with Major Moreau and the officers at the Pentagon, who had attempted to alter his decision.

President Truman sits forward with his elbows on his legs, rolling his glass between his open hands back and forth, thinking. It is several moments before he is prepared to respond.

"I'm impressed with the maturity of your thinking. How old are you?"

"Nineteen, Mr. President."

143

"Very impressed. I suppose many have told you that the award is supposed to inspire others to fight bravely, not just reward you for yours."

"Yes, sir. But, as I said, you wouldn't be rewarding bravery."

The President waves him off.

"I understand. You've stated your case very clearly, and it would be disrespectful to argue with you further."

Truman pauses and stares intently at Nick.

"If nothing else, I want to treat you with all the respect you deserve."

"Thank you, Mr. President, as I wish to treat you. The weight you carry is far more than anyone can understand."

Nick's words move the President to stand and walk to the fireplace, where he leans on the mantle with one hand and stares at the fire as though hiding the emotion in his eyes.

"Thank you for that, son. Truly, thank you."

Truman collects himself and turns to face Nick with a different message.

"However, I have a favor to ask."

"Anything, Mr. President, but..."

The President holds up a hand, ordering Nick to wait and hear him out.

"I need you to accept the Croix de Guerre."

"Mr. President..."

"Hear me out."

"Yes, sir."

"I believe that there's a line of reasoning that may persuade you to accept it."

Nick waits respectfully, doubting.

"The Croix isn't being awarded for bravery."

"But... It isn't?"

"No, it's being awarded for saving the beloved general."

"Pardon me, sir. Don't you mean Colonel Monclar."

"No, he's..."

Truman walks to his desk and shuffles through some papers. He begins reading as he walks back to the fireplace.

"He's General Raoul Charles Magrin-Vernerey. Monclar is a *nom de guerre*."

"A *nom de guerre*."

"An assumed name used in war. The French would only commit to supporting the war in Korea with a battalion. A general can't command a battalion, especially if he's going to be attached to a regiment commanded by a colonel. He changed his name and assumed the rank of lieutenant colonel."

"He wanted to make sure the battalion served with honor."

"What's that?"

"I'm sorry for interrupting, Mr. President."

"No, no. Go ahead."

"The French are embarrassed by their failure to fight honorably during World War II, and he wanted to make sure the Foreign Legion battalion restored their honor."

"And you know this, how?"

"I am friends with the General's adjutant, Major Moreau. He told me."

Truman raises his eyebrows in surprise.

"I'm not surprised that is the case. I'm simply surprised he would admit it."

Truman pours another glass for himself and holds it up to Nick.

"No, thank you, sir. I'd better keep my wits about me. I'm new at this."

The President smiles and nods.

"I'm not."

Truman sits in the wingback chair opposite Nick's and leans forward, causing Nick to lean in sympathy as in a meeting of two conspirators.

"This General is a very popular man. Even President de Gaulle likes him, and he's not an easy man to get along with. The award isn't being awarded for bravery. It's being awarded for saving him. Do you get my drift?"

Nick nods his understanding.

"Good. Now, de Gaulle is trying to restore France's colonial holdings in Southeast Asia, and things aren't going well for him. He wants his allies to help, and we're none too happy to oblige him. That's making him angry, and he may want to drive wedges into the alliance. We can't have that happening, can we?"

"No, sir."

"If you accept the Croix de Guerre, we might be able to trade on your popularity with the people to soften any blow that de Gaulle may be tempted to deliver."

"I see, sir."

"Do you, really?"

"Yes, sir."

"Then you'll accept their award."

Nick doesn't hesitate.

"Yes, Mr. President, I'll accept it."

Truman stands offering his hand to Nick, who stands with him.

Nick wonders if it would be polite to step towards the door, as if to suggest his audience with the President was at an end, when he remembers one last thing he wanted to discuss.

"Mr. President, if I may."

"Certainly."

"Have you heard of the incident at No Gun Ri?"

Trumans face clouds.

"Yes, what of it?"

"I've met one of the men involved, a corporal from the 7th Cavalry.

"Yes, MacArthur's favorites."

"I've also come into possession of eyewitness testimony concerning the incident."

"Whose?"

"Survivors, Mr. President."

"Survivors?"

"Yes, sir. An old woman and some children. Corporal Hatfield, Tommy Hatfield."

"Thomas?"

"I'm not sure, sir."

"You say he was involved?"

"Yes, Mr. President. He was a machine gunner who fired on the refugees."

Truman's face hardens and doesn't soften again until Nick completes his narrative.

#

CHAPTER TWENTY-SEVEN

Family and Friends

Nick's family and friends – the Regans, Dr. Karl and Emma -- step into *The Lafayette*, the grand dining room of the Hay-Adams, just across Lafayette Square from the White House. Chandeliers sparkle above like suspended constellations, casting golden light over white-linen tables and polished silver. The staff moves with quiet precision, dressed in formal black and white, offering menus embossed with gold leaf. Through tall arched windows, the North Lawn is visible in silhouette, the soft glow of the Executive Mansion beyond.

Crystal glasses chime as a sommelier presents the wine, and waiters serve Chesapeake rockfish with saffron Beurre Blanc, dry-aged beef tenderloin, and heirloom vegetables plated like art. Conversations are low and dignified, punctuated by the distant hum of the Capitol's evening. It's the kind of place where senators dine with foreign ministers, and family legacy is celebrated with foie gras and flan de coco. Here, in the quiet elegance of *The Lafayette*, history doesn't just live across the street — it lingers at every table.

Nick's mother and brother walk among the diners like tourists visiting the big city for the first time. Emma Regan, a Baltimore socialite and heiress, is their tour guide, unabashedly introducing Nick, the war hero, and his family to various dignitaries she recognizes. Karl, a noted pediatrician, follows them like an indulgent parent.

The Regans, members of the Baltimore Yacht Club, where Nick's Sea Scout crew also moor their boats, adopted Nick as a crewman and a playmate for their niece, who visits frequently from Cuba, where she lives with her father, who owns a sugar plantation next to the plantation Emma inherited from her grandfather.

Nick's father is conspicuously absent. Emma can't abide the man for his cruelty to Nick. More than once, she's offered to foot the bill for Nick's mother to divorce the man, but divorce isn't socially acceptable in 1950s America.

Nick is forced to recount every detail of his meeting with the President over *hors d'oeuvres*.

Emma almost chokes on her wine when Nick reveals that he will be going to Paris to accept his award of the Croix de Guerre for saving the life of General Vernerey.

"You saved Raoul? Oh my God, Karl. Did you hear that? He saved Raoul Vernerey."

"Yes, dear."

"We must go with you. Please tell us we're invited."

"I don't know if I can invite anyone. It will be a state affair."

"Nick, please. I can get an invitation to any state function. It's your invitation I want. This is your event. I only need to know if you want Karl and me there when you are honored."

"Well, of course, I'd..."

"There! It's done."

Emma turns to Nick's family members.

"And you must attend too. That's okay, isn't it, Nicolas?"

"I'm not sure..."

"Money is no object. The State Department will fly us all, and I'll take care of everything else. They'll put you up in the embassy, or you can join us in our suite at the Ritz Paris."

Karl smiles at his wife as a man in love and shrugs to Nick and his family.

"You may as well allow Emma her ways. She won't be happy unless we're all happy."

After much cajoling, Nick is forced to recount all his adventures in Korea, at least those he remembers, including his association with the refugees from No Gun Ri.

Emma is the first to announce her displeasure.

"That's absolutely deplorable. I hope they've all been punished severely."

"Likely, most are dead. The poorly trained and poorly led don't last long in war."

As the party awaits dessert, Emma senses that Nick is holding back something.

"What is it, Nicolas?"

"There's a group of refugees – an old woman and a group of orphaned children – from No Gun Ri.

There's also a young doctor, educated in America at the Catholic Church's expense. They're living in the shell of an old Catholic Mission south of Seoul. They need the mission reopened and financially secured. Do you think your friend the Cardinal could arrange something?"

"I know he'll arrange something, especially if I endow it."

"I couldn't ask."

"You didn't. I offered."

∞

The party walks back to their hotel to burn off some calories and settle the rest more comfortably. Emma walks with her arm hooked around Nick's while Karl engages Nick's mother and brother in conversation.

Emma's smile betrays pleasant memories.

"What are you thinking about?"

"Raoul."

"Careful. Your husband's just there."

"Posh. Raoul came before Karl."

"You had a…"

"We really must work on your vocabulary if you're going to be stationed in Paris."

Nick blushes.

"The upper crust of European families, especially titled families, were always hunting for rich American girls to marry their sons and salvage the family fortunes."

"General Vernerey's was such a family?"

"But, of course."

Emma changes the topic to avoid shocking Nick any further.

"What are your plans?"

"What do you mean?"

"Well, let's start easy. What's next after you receive your award?"

"I'm traveling to Nepal."

"Nepal! How exotic."

"I'm going to be adopted by Limbu's family."

"How many families can adopt one person?"

"I don't know if there's a limit."

"Why do you want to be adopted by them?"

"It's not really a matter of what I want. It's..."

"Tradition?"

"Yes."

"I think I understand. And after that?"

"I have to go back to Korea."

"What?! Haven't you done enough for the war?"

"No, I'm not going to rejoin my unit there. In fact, I've been assigned to the Embassy in Paris."

"Exciting! How's your French?"

"Quite good, I've been told. A friend started my lessons, and he's an excellent teacher."

"He? A woman should teach a man French."

Nick smiles at his benefactor.

"Well, you're not a teenager anymore."

"Actually, I am."

"Well, maybe chronologically, but you're a man now, I'm sure. You are a man now, aren't you?"

"Whatever do you mean?"

Emma and Nick walk the rest of the way to the hotel in silence, broken only by intermittent snickering.

#

CHAPTER TWENTY-EIGHT

The Hidden Goodbye

Tommy grabs his bugout bag and escapes to the countryside when the children sound the alarm.

"Soldiers are coming!"

He runs to a low rise that shows him a clear line of sight back to the mission, where he sees a small convoy of military vehicles, several trucks with a jeep at the front and rear of the column, approaching. His muscles tense when he sees them stop and soldiers disembark. They aren't communist. The vehicles are all American, though the markings aren't. Even though he can't read, he can tell there is something different about them. Each door is stenciled with a large "UN."

There are three trucks – 2 – 2-1/2-ton cargo/troop haulers and a dump truck – and two jeeps – each equipped with a pylon mounting a light machine gun.

Nick steps out of the lead jeep and orders the soldiers in well-spoken French to disperse and secure the area. He pauses for several moments, scanning the old mission and its outbuildings, looking for signs of life. There is none to be seen when they arrive. The children have hidden themselves in cellars and culverts nearby.

Nick isn't fooled. He can see smoke rising from a chimney. There are signs of repairs. It's apparent that Tommy has been hard at work. Roofs are patched with tiles fashioned from wood. Doors are back on their hinges. And there's a playground fashioned from barrels and pipes that Tommy scavenged from God knows where, and ingeniously joined into swing sets, teeter totters, slides, and climbing apparatus.

An old nun emerges from the main building and approaches Nick with a confident step. She examines the young American officer and his French Legionnaire companions.

"You must be Nick. I'm Mother Superior Agnes."

The old nun is obviously Korean, and Nick responds in the language that Soon-Ja taught him. He switches to English at the nun's request.

"Is Soon-Ja here?"

Sister Agnes smiles sadly.

"I'm sorry, Lieutenant. I can't help you with that.

"She's not here."

She shrugs but remains mute.

"Is she just away or did she leave?"

Sister Agnes remains as still and as mute as a statue.

"Is Henry here?"

"He left when he saw your trucks approaching."

"When will he return?"

"Probably not until you're gone."

"That's too bad. I don't suppose it would help if I went to look for him."

The Mother Superior nods. "Probably not. You wouldn't get close enough for him to recognize you."

"Then you must know why."

"Yes, I know the story."

The two are interrupted momentarily when the Legionnaire sergeant approaches to report that the area is clear. Nick thanks him and orders a break for the men until he can decide where they should offload the supplies.

Sister Agnes voices her surprise.

"Interesting that an American officer is leading a group of French soldiers."

"I'm not in charge, exactly. They were loaned to me to help scrounge supplies and deliver them so that you can subsist until a regular flow of supplies is established."

"And where will these supplies come from?"

Nick hands the nun a letter.

"You can read this at your leisure, but in summary, this mission has been adopted by the archdiocese of Baltimore, Maryland, and will receive financial support from them in perpetuity. I'll explain in more detail later. First, let's get these trucks unloaded. We have clothing, bedding, and foodstuffs. And, as you can see, a dump truck full of coal."

The nun is taken aback but recovers quickly.

"The coal can be dumped in the bunker there between the kitchen and the dormitory. The food can be taken to the kitchen. Sister Monica is there to provide direction if the men want to help her put it away. Have everything else put in the dormitory over there. We'll sort that out later."

"Very well."

Nick calls for the sergeant and provides him with Mother Superior's requests. The sergeant salutes and hurries to start the offloading.

"Please thank the men for me."

"You may do that yourself. All speak English as well."

"But you speak to them in French."

"I suppose I'm just showing off as much as practicing. I've been studying French for only a few months."

"Only a few months and you speak it so well. Of course, I don't speak it myself, but it sounds as though you are fluent in your use of it."

An awkward silence descends between them as Nick looks about.

"As I said, I can't help you."

Nick takes a deep breath and allows it to escape in a sigh.

"I had hoped…"

"Can I offer refreshments?"

"Please allow my men to prepare the meal. You won't be disappointed. I haven't met a Frenchman yet who isn't an excellent cook, and they brought some treats that the children should enjoy. Where are they?"

"Hiding. Come, we'll call them."

The Mother Superior leads Nick to the chapel entrance and instructs him to pull the bell rope. Children begin emerging from their warrens on the very first ring. They surround the soldiers with hands outstretched to receive candy.

Nick calls the sergeant to join him, and the nun leads them to the kitchen. Nick and the sergeant confer briefly and separate with a salute.

"You need a proper larder, Mother Superior. We can stay until tomorrow and build one."

"I suppose Tommy will survive the night."

∞

Nick and Mother Superior sit in her office that evening, sharing tea and a French pastry prepared by one of the soldiers that afternoon. The mood between them is mellow as candlelight softly bathes the room.

"Funds have been deposited to a branch of Bank of America in Seoul."

Nick hands her a business card.

"This is the bank officer who has been designated to assist you with whatever you need. He'll visit you next week to help write a budget, provide you with a checkbook, and whatever else you need. It'll be a while before postal or telephone service reaches this far outside Seoul, so he's promised to make regular trips to check up on you and the children and see to your needs."

Nick provides Mother Superior with a printed manifest of the supplies they have delivered.

"Two milk cows, some goats, and chickens will be delivered next week."

"Now that is a Godsend, bless you."

"There will also be feed. The men will build sheds and enclosures for all tomorrow."

"That's a lot to do in one day."

Nick replies with a shrug.

"They can do it."

Nick then delivers a letter that Emma gave him in Paris before he left for Nepal.

"This is from your benefactor, Emma Regan. It outlines the details of the line of credit that her private foundation has arranged for you beyond the provisions of the Baltimore Archdiocese. There are thousands of orphans all over Korea, and many are bound to show up on your doorstep."

The old nun nods in agreement.

"Sadly, yes."

She puts the letter aside after reading it and looks frankly into Nick's eyes.

"How does the war go?"

"It's a stalemate. It seems that the line separating North and South Korea will be restored at the 38th Parallel."

"All that fighting and death for nothing, then?"

"Yes."

Another silence passes between them before Nick continues.

"President Truman is taking this very badly."

"He is?"

"Yes, he believes that it is his fault.

The Mother Superior raises her eyebrows but says nothing as she waits to hear more.

"Shortly before the war, he allowed his Secretary of State to make a public statement that the communists interpreted as American reluctance to defend South Korea. He believes that it encouraged them to launch this misadventure."

The Mother Superior nods.

"It is never good to show weakness to a bully."

"Yes, he prays that no President will ever again make that mistake."

"I'm told there was another man with you."

"Yes, Limbu Wotman. A Gurkha."

"What happened to him?"

"He died when we raided a Chinese headquarters."

"We will pray for him."

"Thank you, Mother Superior. What of the old woman? Does she still harass poor Tommy?"

The old nun shifts in her chair and attempts to look stern, but a chuckle and a smile escapes.

"I put an end to that, but she still hits him when she thinks I'm not looking and feels that Tommy isn't penitent enough."

Nick hands the nun another letter, this one addressed to Tommy.

"Please see that he gets this."

∞

On the morning of the second day following their arrival, the troops are loaded into their trucks. Before mounting his jeep, Nick turns to Mother Superior and hands one more envelope to her. It's addressed simply "Soon-Ja".

"If you ever see her again."

"I'll make sure she gets it."

"Thank you."

With children running alongside, the small convoy exits the mission compound and drives away in a cloud of dust.

#

CHAPTER TWENTY-SEVEN

Farewell

Soon-Ja stands at the window in Mother Superior's office, watching the convoy disappear in the distance. The nun sits at her desk, busying herself with some papers, occasionally stealing a glance at the young woman.

Nick's convoy is long gone before Soon-Ja takes a seat across the desk from the nun, who watches her carefully.

"He loves you."

"I know."

"I believe you love him."

"I did. I suppose I always will."

"He would marry you."

"I know."

"Why did you hide?"

"He's not ready."

The nun looks closely at Soon-Ja, patiently waiting for an explanation.

"Nick has a demon within him. It will take time for him to tame it."

"All men wrestle with demons."

Soon-Ja coughs on a laugh and smiles at the older woman dressed in the habit of one married to Christ.

"Yes, I suppose they do, but none as strong as Nick's."

Mother Superior rings a tiny bell on her desk that is answered by a novice working in the anteroom.

"Tea?"

"Yes, please."

The nun returns to her papers. When she looks up, Soon-Ja is rubbing her belly.

"He's kicking?"

Soon-Ja smiles.

"Yes, he's a strong one."

"Nick would have made a good father."

"Maybe, someday."

"Don't you think he should know?"

Soon-Ja focuses on her swollen belly as she considers the nun's question.

"No, he would only torment himself. Seeing that I'm pregnant would force him to choose between his destiny and mine, and that wouldn't be fair."

The nun is about to argue when a soft rap sounds at the door.

"Come in, Tommy."

The nun's command is answered promptly by the appearance of the soldier dressed in a monk's robes. He carries the tea service for the two women.

"Why didn't you bring a cup for yourself?"

"No, thank you, ma'am."

Tommy watches out the window as if expecting the soldiers to return.

"He's gone."

"Will they be back?"

"No."

"Too bad. I'd like to have seen him."

"He wanted to see you."

"Hmmm."

Mother Superior extends her hand with the letter that Nick had delivered.

"He brought this for you."

Tommy looks at it blankly, turning it every which way after accepting it.

"Who's it from?"

"The President."

"Of the United States?"

"Yes, Tommy. Would you like me to read it to you?"

"Yes, please, ma'am."

Sister Agnes and Soon-Ja share a quick glance and a smile as the nun opens the envelope, taking care not to rip it.

"You'll want to save this, I'm sure."

"Yes, ma'am."

Mother Superior's glasses hang from a lanyard around her neck. She sets the letter down as she cleans and puts them on. Tommy waits patiently for her to begin reading.

"To Thomas Hatfield, Corporal, United States Army

"Greetings

"Dear Tommy

"I have received the testimony of Lieutenant Nicolas Andrews in the case of the events at No Gun

Ri, Korea, on 26 July to 29 July 1950, and your part in them.

"Although lawyers would complain that his comments are inadmissible in court under the Hearsay Rule, I believe they are sufficient to guide me in disposing of this matter.

"In all fairness, I cannot forgive you for your role in the massacre of so many innocent civilians, men, women, and children. Forgiveness is a matter that I must leave to you and God, as well as the victims of the crimes mentioned.

"However, inasmuch as Lieutenant Andrews has described in great and articulate detail the self-imposed penance that you have been serving, I do not believe that it will serve the interests of justice for the United States government to punish you further.

"I am pleased that you have not attempted to defend your actions by claiming that you were acting under the orders of your superior officers. We have only recently concluded trials of Nazis at Nuremberg, where such a defense was dismissed repeatedly. No one, regardless of rank, is obligated to obey unlawful orders, and firing upon unarmed noncombatants is the greatest example of an unlawful order as I can imagine.

"Therefore, it is my determination that you shall have my pardon and that you will not be persecuted nor prosecuted further for these crimes should you return to the jurisdiction of this nation.

"Furthermore, I have caused the Secretary of Defense to issue to you a Discharge from Service in the United States Army Under Other Than Honorable Conditions. I hope that you appreciate the fact that you cannot be accorded the full rights and privileges enjoyed by veterans who have served honorably.

"Signed, Harry S. Truman, President of the United States and Command-in-Chief of the Armed Forces of the United States."

Mother Superior folds the letter carefully when she finishes and returns it to its envelope.

"I imagine that you will want to keep this in a safe place."

Tommy hesitates to accept the letter.

"You may wish to keep it inside your Bible."

"Yes, ma'am. Thank you, ma'am."

He accepts it with both hands.

Soon-Ja takes one of Tommy's hands and places it on her stomach so that he can feel the baby kicking.

"Will you be his uncle?"

A great smile forms slowly on Tommy's face.

"Yes, ma'am!"

"You can help me teach him how to read."

Tommy responds with a bewildered look.

"Of course, we'll have to teach you first."

Soon-Ja winks, and Tommy's smile returns.

Mother Superior waits for Soon-Ja and Tommy to leave her office before she removes Nick's card from her sleeve and reads the message he has written.

"Please write when you get this. Address the letter to my friends, Dr. and Mrs. Karl Regan. I love you. Nick."

Following the message is the Regan's address.

The old nun turns the card over in her hand front-to-back several times. After a few moments, she sighs and unlocks a drawer from which she removes a small wooden box and drops the card inside. She then returns the box to the drawer and relocks it.

###

AFTERWARD

The True Cost of War

In revisiting The Accidental Spy *for this second edition, it is fitting to reflect not only on the historical backdrop of espionage, strategy, and sacrifice — but also on the staggering cost in civilian lives that too often remains obscured beneath the fog of war and the veil of time.*

The Korean War, frequently labeled "The Forgotten War," exacted a horrifying toll on the civilian population of the Korean Peninsula. Estimates suggest that as many as 2 to 3 million Korean civilians perished between 1950 and 1953. This represents approximately 10% of the total Korean population at the time — a figure that stands among the highest civilian casualty rates in any modern conflict.

To place that in historical context: during the entirety of World War II, one of the deadliest conflicts in human history, no major participating nation suffered a proportional civilian loss on this scale. The Soviet Union, with the highest total civilian toll, lost an estimated 13–14 million noncombatants — but that equated to about 7–8% of its prewar population. Poland, including the Jewish victims of the Holocaust, suffered civilian losses approaching 17% — a figure that, while higher, was tied to both conventional warfare and systematic genocide. The most astounding of all is the wartime experience of Japan which suffered the loss of 1.5% of its civilian population despite the devastation of Tokyo by firebombing and Hiroshima and Nagasaki by atomic bombs.

By contrast, the Korean War's devastation came from aerial bombardment, artillery barrages, scorched-earth tactics, and widespread displacement. Entire cities were razed. Civilian refugees were caught between two advancing and retreating armies, often deliberately targeted or deemed expendable. Villages suspected of aiding the enemy were strafed, bombed, or burned. Both the North and South Korean regimes, as well as foreign armies, committed atrocities in the name of ideology and security.

That such a price was paid in so brief a conflict — just three years — should weigh heavily on our historical conscience.

It is through stories like The Accidental Spy, though fictionalized, that we attempt to humanize these statistics and remember the individuals who lived, suffered, and died in the shadows of geopolitics. As we examine history through the lens of one soldier's experience, we are reminded that every war, however "limited" in scope or forgotten in memory, leaves behind an unlimited grief etched in the lives of civilians who never volunteered for battle.

Let this second edition serve not only as a narrative of espionage, duty, and survival, but also as

*a solemn acknowledgment of the true cost of war —
one measured not only in fallen soldiers, but also in
families shattered and generations lost.*

The End

THE NICK ANDREWS SERIES

Book 2: The Reluctant Spy
2nd Edition

In the shadow of the Cold War, U.S. Army officer Nick Andrews is sent into Hungary under diplomatic cover. His mission: observe the rising tension behind the Iron Curtain and report back. No interference. No engagement. Just eyes and ears.

But Budapest in 1956 is on the verge of revolution. The people — students, workers, and soldiers alike — are demanding freedom from Soviet rule. As the uprising erupts into open rebellion, Nick is drawn deeper into a world of betrayal, sacrifice, and impossible choices.

Masquerading as a French trade negotiator, Nick navigates secret police, Soviet tanks, and underground resistance cells. With every step, he risks blowing his cover—or worse, his soul. When the revolution ignites, he must choose -- walk away or fight alongside those who refuse to kneel.

He came as a spy. He stays as a revolutionary.

THE NICK ANDREWS SERIES

Book 3: The Last Spy
2nd Edition

In 1956, U.S. Army Captain Nick Andrews is sent to Havana to calm American nerves. Washington wants to believe Cuba is stable. Business interests demand reassurance. The Mafia counts on uninterrupted profits. Nick's job: confirm that the island remains in friendly hands.

But what he finds is a nation on the edge — its people restless, its leader corrupt, and a quiet revolution already rising in the shadows. As idealist Fidel Castro sails toward Cuba's eastern shore, Nick tracks him across land and sea, even as his growing bond with Lucia Comas, a Cuban heiress, draws him deeper into the island's fate.

Nick sounds the alarm. Washington doesn't listen. And when the U.S. interferes anyway, it triggers the very uprising it meant to avoid.

Caught between duty and truth, love and loyalty, Nick must choose which side of history he's willing to stand on — before Cuba burns.

About the Author

Jack Durish is a decorated veteran, a sailor, and a grandfather, the makings of a great storyteller. He was raised on the Chesapeake Bay, where he began a lifelong love of adventure that led him to explore more exotic locales, including Hawaii, California, and Colorado. Jack enlisted in the Army at the height of the Vietnam War and earned his commission as a second lieutenant at the Infantry Officer Candidate School at Fort Benning, Georgia. He served with the 9th Infantry Division, where he experienced the thrill and horror of war. During this time, he investigated and reported on three actions that resulted in awards of the Medal of Honor, giving him deep insight into the character of valor and heroism.

You can find his work and reflections at jackdurish.com.